The Books of Nancy Moser

www.nancymoser.com

Contemporary Books

An Undiscovered Life

Eyes of Our Heart

The Invitation (Book 1 Mustard Seed)

The Quest (Book 2 Mustard Seed)

The Temptation (Book 3 Mustard Seed)

Crossroads

The Seat Beside Me (Book 1 Steadfast)

A Steadfast Surrender (Book Steadfast)

The Ultimatum (Book 3 Steadfast)

The Sister Circle (Book 1 Sister Circle)

Round the Corner (Book 2 Sister Circle)

An Undivided Heart (Book 3 Sister Circle)

A Place to Belong (Book 4 Sister Circle)

The Sister Circle Handbook (Book 5 Sister Circle)

Time Lottery (Book 1 Time Lottery)

Second Time Around (Book 2 Time Lottery)

John 3:16

The Good Nearby

Solemnly Swear

Save Me, God! I Fell in the Carpool (Inspirational humor)

100 Verses of Encouragement — Books 1&2 (illustrated gift books)

Maybe Later (picture book)

I Feel Amazing: the ABCs of Emotion (picture book)

D1598294

The Bridal Quilt

ISBN 13: 978-1-7368108-5-9

Published by:
Mustard Seed Press
Overland Park, KS

This story is a work of fiction. Any resemblances to actual people, places, or events are purely coincidental.

All Scripture quotations are taken from The Holy Bible, King James Version.

Front cover design by Mustard Seed Press

Printed and bound in the United States of America

The
Bridal Quilt

NANCY MOSER

Overland Park, KS

Chapter One

New York City, November 1889

"But Samuel, you *can't* leave me alone tonight." Ada stood within the warmth of his arms and fingered his diamond tie tack. "My evenings are empty when we're not together."

Samuel took her busy hands captive. "As are mine, dear lady. Your companionship is always my first choice."

"Then why—?"

"My friends know how devoted we are to each other. So much so, that they insist I pull myself away for a Friday evening in their company."

Ada knew the young men in their set didn't like how she'd plucked Samuel out of their circle. She imagined they were a bit uneasy to witness the effects of true love, especially when they would rather concentrate on flirtation, frivolity, and fun. They were mere boys, while her Samuel was a man.

Her man.

The clock on the parlor's mantel struck eight, causing Samuel to press his lips to hers before gathering his hat and cloak. "I'll call on you tomorrow at one. Would you like to go to the Met? We could dine afterward."

That sounded delightful. But Ada didn't want to let him off so easily. "Are you certain one is late enough after your night carousing with the boys?"

He volleyed her teasing right back at her. "One fifteen then." With a wink he left her.

The room was empty without him.

But before Ada could brood, she heard the tinkle of a bell coming from upstairs. Nana needed her.

Ada met her mother in the upper hallway. She was also on the way to answer the summons.

"I'll go, Mother."

"But Samuel. . ."

"He left." Mother looked taken aback, so Ada explained. "He had another engagement." When her mother's eyebrows rose, she added, "We aren't engaged yet, so Samuel is free to. . .to. . ."

"He's been so attentive, Ada. You must see to it this match is made. The Alcott banking fortune is huge and—"

"I wouldn't be marrying Samuel for his money. We love each other."

"All the better. But you really must—"

Her grandmother's bell saved her. "If you'll excuse me."

"Get him to propose, dear," Mother said. "Samuel Alcott is an excellent catch."

Ada was glad she was walking away so she could roll her eyes without fear of a reprimand. Yes, yes, she knew Samuel was an excellent catch, and yes, she would like nothing better than for him to propose. But her mother's words cheapened the feelings they had for each other. For this wasn't some arranged match; it was true love. Samuel could have been a peddler on the street and she wouldn't love him less. They were soul mates.

She cherished any time they spent together, whether it was going to the opera, enjoying dinner at the Vanderbilts', or sitting before the fire reading to each other. *How do I love thee? Let me count the ways. . . .*

Ada couldn't count the ways she loved Samuel. Each smile, each word, each wink, each touch left her feeling—*knowing*—that their love was a gift from God.

A proposal would come soon. Samuel had hinted at a special surprise he had planned for her at Christmas, which was just a month away. Marriage was inevitable, and a lifetime together was a dream that would come true.

Ada knocked softly on the door to her grandmother's room, then entered. The gas sconces were unlit, the only light coming from an oil lamp on the bedside table. Ada sought Nana's face. She could always tell how she was feeling by her expression. This evening there was an absence of discomfort, but her brow was furrowed. "What's wrong?" Ada asked, taking her hand. "You seem worried."

"I heard the front door open, then close in only thirty minutes' time. Why did Samuel leave you so soon?"

Ada smiled. Although loss of hearing was a normal result of age, Nana's hearing was finely tuned. Even though she often felt poorly, she knew the comings and goings in the Wallace household almost better than those who experienced them firsthand.

"Samuel's friends are jealous of the time he spends with me and insist he spend time with them tonight." Ada perched on the chair beside the bed, her bustle preventing her from sitting back.

"Can you blame them?" Nana said. "They know they're losing one of their own to the matrimonial yoke."

"That's a horrible term, Nana."

She shrugged. "To men it fits. To most men, anyway. They mourn the loss of their freedom, even as they seek marriage for its social advantages and the private. . .benefits."

Ada felt herself blush. Her mother would never even elude to the intimate side of marriage, so she was glad for Nana's more direct manner. "Samuel's not like that."

"Oh, I guarantee you, he is — and be glad for it. For without those advantages and benefits — especially the private ones — marriage is as shallow as a pond in a dry spell."

Ada was glad her mother wasn't in the room to cringe at Nana's down-home sayings. Nana had married well and had risen from her meager station to become a matriarch within New York society's "Four Hundred"—the elite of the elite. Mother seemed to have forgotten that fact, and that most of their friends—including the Vanderbilts and the Astors—had also started low and ended high after they came to America. Nana said that having dirt on your shoes didn't matter if you were on the right path.

Her proverbs always made Ada smile. Mother, on the other hand, wished there'd been an additional generation between their current wealth and Nana's humble beginnings.

Nana pointed to Ada's sewing basket. "Go gather your quilt-work and let's have a good talk."

"But didn't you need something?"

"I needed to have a good talk with *you*. Now go on. Idle hands are the devil's workshop."

Ada retrieved her sewing basket and took out the latest block of the crazy quilt she was making for her trousseau. She'd been working on it for six years, since she'd turned thirteen. Each fabric corresponded to a dress she'd worn and brought back memories of people and places and happy occasions. It was her bridal quilt, a map of her life she would bring to a marriage, detailing her life *before*. Once married, she would start a new quilt to chronicle that season of her life.

This particular square was nearly finished, with just some embroidery needed across the seemingly haphazard array of pieces. She threaded her needle with sage-green floss.

Nana pointed to the color. "That green against your mauve silk is a pretty choice. You do have an eye for such things."

"I take after you."

"Of course you do." Nana smoothed her gnarled hands over the lace edging on the sheet. "Now then. To the subject at hand. I won't ask if Samuel's proposed, because I know I'd be the first to know." She looked at Ada over her glasses, challenging her.

"Who else would I tell first?"

"Your mother."

Ada knew there was tension between Nana and Mother — but tried not to take sides or play into it. "Mother will definitely be next."

"Hmm."

Ada changed the subject. "Samuel's taking me to the art museum tomorrow."

"Say hello to the paintings for me. Did you know you and I were there when it opened?"

"Yes, Nana." Ada had heard her grandmother's story of the first reception of the Metropolitan Museum of Art in 1870. How they'd hung the initial 174 paintings covering the walls from floor to ceiling, causing Nana to comment that obviously a woman needed stilts to see the paintings properly, eye to eye. Ada had only been a baby, but Nana had prided herself on starting her art education early. She'd always been the one to take Ada and her brother, John, on outings. Ada's fondest memories were of the times spent as the Three Musketeers, seeing New York through Nana's eyes. How sad those times were over. Nana rarely ventured out of bed anymore, though her illnesses were often vague.

Ada's face must have revealed her wistfulness, but Nana guessed wrongly about the cause. "Don't you go worrying about Samuel going out with his friends. If

12

you don't trust his character, you shouldn't consider marrying the man."

"Oh, I trust him. I just don't trust his friends."

"Now there, I can't help you. Let's say a prayer that God does the watching for us."

Amen.

**

"Come on, Samuel. Don't tell us you've never gone slumming." Joseph yanked on his arm.

Samuel nearly tripped on the cobblestones, then righted himself and gently pushed his drunken friend away. It had been good to catch up on the news and latest gossip, but two hours and far too many drinks later on his friends' part, and Samuel was done with it. And now they wanted to go down to Five Points — to the immigrant slums? Nothing good could come of it.

But then Leo whistled for a hack and dragged Samuel inside while the other three shoved from behind.

"To the slums, driver! Show us how the other half lives!" Oscar was the last one in the carriage, and virtually fell over Samuel on the way to his seat. When he muttered, "Sorry, old chum," his breath smelled of onions, garlic, and wine.

I gave up time with Ada for this? Samuel turned away from his friends to stare out the window. *Sweet, kind, bright, curious Ada.* How he loved her. Why hadn't he proposed yet? She was expecting it and he wanted to oblige.

But something was holding him back.

There was no way he could explain his hesitation to her—he had trouble explaining it to himself. Was it the voice of God, or simply his own inability to make a decision? Maybe it wasn't anything to be concerned about. After all, didn't everyone feel apprehension when making a life-changing decision?

He closed his eyes a moment and said an oft-repeated prayer. *Show me Your will, O Lord.* Over the years he'd come to know this prayer covered everything. He could pray for specifics, spelling out exactly what *he* wanted, but in the end, it came down to preferring God's plan over his own. He couldn't pinpoint any monumental moment when he'd officially deferred to God's will, as the habit had evolved over a lifetime of being the son of parents who lived their faith. And a grandmother.

His parents had died when he was eleven, back on Christmas Day 1876. At least they'd been together. At least they'd been doing what they loved to do—attending the theater. That the theater had burned, killing nearly three hundred people, had been a horrific end to a happy day. But for a bad cough, Samuel would have been in the theater with them. "You were saved for something, Samuel," was a mantra oft-repeated by his dear grandmother, who, with Grandfather, had raised him. He felt it was his duty to find out exactly what that *something* was.

Grandmother had been gone four years now, but she'd always encouraged him by saying, "Listen for the Lord—whether it be a whisper or a shout."

Samuel had never heard God shout, but he'd come to believe the whispers in his mind were God's way of directing him to do the right thing. And so, until the *"Wait"* was replaced with a *"Now!"* Samuel would bide his time proposing to Ada.

Yet he sorely wished God would give him the go-ahead soon. How he longed to make her happy.

The carriage came to a stop and Samuel's friends looked outside and loudly made the determination that they had, indeed, arrived in the slums.

Leo pressed some coins in the driver's hand and said, "Wait for us. We'll be back in a—"

The driver shook his head. "Pardon me, sir, but I ain't waiting 'ere for no man."

"Then how—?"

The driver pulled away, leaving them standing on the dark street.

Joseph laughed nervously. "Well then, chums. It appears we're on our own to explore."

"Explore some'ere else," came a voice.

They looked to the entrance of an alley and saw a man curled in a ball, trying to sleep on the ground.

He glared up at them with a toothless smile and pretended to doff his hat. "If yer don' mind, gen'lemen."

Oscar removed his own hat, swept it into an exaggerated bow, and addressed the man, his words slurred by the drink. "Anythin' you say, your majesty."

The man roused. " 'Ey there. No need to be rude."

No, there wasn't. Samuel pulled Oscar away. "Leave him be."

Oddly, the streets were full of people. It was after eleven, but people—mostly men—lollygagged around the stone steps leading to the front doors of dilapidated tenements, or were seen in the shadows, their hands in their pockets, watching Samuel and company like vultures eyeing their prey.

"I don't think this was a good idea," Joseph said under his breath. "We need to get out of here."

Oscar tipped his hat to the men, and Samuel pulled him forward even harder. "Stop it!" he whispered. "You'll get us all killed."

The sounds of an argument and more than one crying baby could be heard from the windows that looked down upon the narrow street. A dog ate some horse droppings just as someone heaved a pail of rubbish from an upper window.

It splattered on Oscar's shoes. "Ahh!" He looked upward. "What do you think you're doing?"

A woman appeared in the window and yelled something in Italian—complete with hand gestures—before shutting the window with a thud.

Samuel sidestepped around the rubbish—which appeared to be the leftovers of a meal.

A scantily dressed woman emerged from the shadows and locked onto Leo. She spoke in some Slavic language, her features exotic. Her hand brushed across Leo's chest, and suddenly, Leo took her wrist roughly. "Oh no, you don't! Let go of my wallet! And get away with you!" He pushed her away, and she smiled at him smugly, as if his rebuff meant little.

A group of four children suddenly swarmed around them, tugging at the men's clothes, their small hands hunting for some bounty.

"Off! Get away!" Joseph said.

The children scattered, but looking up the street was like viewing a gauntlet to be run. The young men's shouts—their very presence—were drawing too much attention. Samuel pointed back to the way they had come. "Men, we need to leave. Now. Perhaps we can catch a cab if we walk north—"

A child's screams cut through his words, and another kind of instinct took over. Samuel ran toward the scream into an alley. There, in the dim light of the moon, he saw a man hitting a little girl. Slapping her. Shaking her. Tossing her against the alley's debris only to pick her up again for more abuse.

Samuel ran forward. "Stop that! Stop that right now!"

The man paused in midslap. He glared at Samuel. "What's it to you?"

Before Samuel could answer, the girl made a run for it toward the street. Then, obviously spooked by the presence of Samuel's friends, she returned and took refuge behind Samuel. She pointed at the man and said something in another language.

The man picked up a piece of wood and slapped it against his palm. He strode forward slowly. "So this is the way it's gonna be. Don't make no never mind to me whether I hurt her or hurt you. 'Tis your choice, Mr. Fancypants."

"Samuel, come on." It was Oscar.

Samuel couldn't risk looking back to see exactly where his friends were, but by Oscar's voice, Samuel knew they had not followed him into the alley.

They were not supporting him.

"There's a cab at the next intersection!" Leo said. "I'll go hail it."

"Come on, Samuel," Joseph said. "Don't get between a father and his daughter."

"Er ist nicht mein Vater!" the girl said.

The man pointed his weapon at the girl. "You owe me, *Liebchen*, and you'll do as I say, *verstehe*?" He lunged toward her, forcing Samuel to step back, holding the girl in place behind him.

But the man was too quick. He reached around Samuel and grabbed the girl by the sleeve of her coat and yanked her back. He heaved her to the side of the alley where she bounced off the brick wall and fell to the ground in a crumpled heap.

Samuel had never witnessed such cruelty. He took a step toward the girl to help her, but the man moved between them.

"You leave 'er be," the man said. "She's mine!"

Samuel looked at the girl, then the man, then the girl. She moaned and was not getting up.

Oscar called from the street. "Come on, Samuel! The cab's waiting."

Then he had an idea. He reached in his coat pocket where he'd placed the change from dinner and pulled out a handful of coins. It was only a few dollars, but it would have to do. Samuel held the money in his palm. "See here? I have over twenty dollars in coins. For your trouble."

"Now yer talkin'," the man said, taking a step forward.

Samuel flung the coins over the man's head, deeper in the alley where they clattered and scattered. A man who'd been sleeping in the shadows emerged and began scrambling after the money.

"Hey! Stop that! Those are mine!" The evil man raced back to claim his coins.

The distraction was just what Samuel needed. He rushed to the girl, scooped her into his arms, and ran toward the street.

At the mouth of the alley, he turned right and ran as fast as he could, feeling as if the hounds of Hades were nipping at his heels.

"Come on!" shouted Joseph from the cab a block ahead.

Behind him Samuel heard the man take chase.

"Come on! Hurry!"

Once at the cab, Samuel tossed the girl into the arms of his friends and dove in after her. The cab pulled away with his feet still hanging from the door. The sound of the horse's hooves replaced the footsteps of the man.

His friends helped him to a seat. The frightened girl sat on Oscar's lap. Blood glistened on her face, and Samuel retrieved a handkerchief.

As Samuel noticed the blood, so did Oscar. "Eeww. You take her!" He handed her off, then checked the cleanliness of his suit. "Why'd you bring her with you?"

Samuel carefully dabbed at a cut on the girl's forehead, hating to see her wince. She looked at him with wary eyes. What must she be thinking? Even though he'd saved her, she had no reason to trust him. To trust anyone. For all she knew he was simply another kind of evil man. "I suppose you would have left her there?"

Oscar didn't answer.

"She smells awful," Joseph said, holding a handkerchief to his nose.

Samuel was appalled at their reactions. "What's wrong with you? Where is your compassion?"

"I left it in my other suit." Oscar laughed at his own joke.

Their laughter was like acid. Samuel had known these men his entire life — or at least he'd thought he'd known them. How could they be so cold and uncaring?

Finally Leo weighed in. "Chide them all you want, Samuel. The point remains: What are you going to do with her?"

Good question.

**

Samuel would never forget the look on the butler's face when he entered his family's home carrying the girl.

"Mr. Samuel! What happened? Who —?"

"As you can see, Briggs, the girl is injured. I'm taking her to the green bedroom."

"I . . . Should I call for Dr. Brandeis?"

Although Samuel couldn't be sure, he didn't think the girl's injuries were life-threatening. "I don't think that's necessary — at least not yet. Please call Sally to come help."

"Very good, sir," Briggs said.

Samuel headed up the staircase and was pleased when the girl linked her hands around his neck.

"It will be all right," he said to her. "You're safe now."

**

An hour later, Samuel tapped on the door of the green bedroom. Sally, the maid, told him to come in.

He found Sally tucking the girl into bed. She looked like a far different girl than the one he'd seen on the streets. Her hair was light brown, nearly blond, and her face was cleaned of dirt and blood — though there were bruises forming on her cheeks.

"She's all clean, Mister Samuel," Sally said. "I even fed her some of our leftover dinner."

He motioned Sally aside. "What of her injuries?"

Sally kept her voice low. "She's been beaten more than once, with bruises on her limbs and body of every color from red to blue to yellow. But she doesn't seem to have any broken bones." She nodded toward the bed. "I gave her one of your grandmother's old nightgowns and sent her clothes down to be washed. Her coat is barely a coat. It's a wonder she didn't freeze out there. I hope I did right."

"You did well, Sally. You did everything you should have done."

"She doesn't seem to speak any English, sir, but she understands a bit. I think her name is Nusa," Sally said.

The girl nodded and pointed at herself. "Nusa. *Ja.*"

Samuel went to the bedside. "I'm Samuel."

Nusa let loose with a long discourse in what sounded like German. How he wished he knew the language. But then

Nusa stopped talking and looked at the door.

Samuel's grandfather stood there in his dressing gown, taking it all in. "What's all this ruckus in the middle of the night?"

Oh dear. Samuel drew his grandfather into the hall and told him the story of finding the girl.

"So you plucked her off the street?"

"She was being beaten."

"Then save her. But don't bring her here. Where are her parents?"

Samuel realized how little he knew about her. "I don't know."

"Don't you think you'd better find out? They'll be worried about her."

As usual, his grandfather cut right to the chase. The entire series of events had transpired so quickly, Samuel hadn't thought it through. "I'll take her back tomorrow and we'll find them."

"See that you do." With one more glance into the room, his grandfather added, "Is she wearing one of your grandmother's nightgowns?"

"Yes, sir. I—"

Grandfather turned and walked away. Samuel didn't have time to regret his grandfather's disapproval, for he heard Sally clear her throat. "She wants you, sir."

He'd worry about pleasing Grandfather another day.

Nusa needed him.

Chapter Two

"Careful now, John," Ada told her brother.

"Nana knows she's safe with me," John said as he helped their grandmother down the stairs to the parlor. "Or maybe she'd prefer to slide down the banister." He moved to lift Nana atop the heavy oak railing, but Nana flicked his ear.

"If my bones were a few decades younger, I'd take you up on that, Johnny."

Ada hurried ahead and got the pillows on the fainting couch ready. John helped Nana to her place, and Ada arranged the folds of her dressing gown, adding a velvet coverlet over her legs.

"There now," Nana said. "I'm snug as a bug in a rug."

"Can I get you anything?" John asked.

"Not a thing. When I have you and Ada in my presence, I am totally content."

The feelings were reciprocated. The world was a safe and even place with Nana around.

John checked his pocket watch. "I do have a little time before I need to leave for the Academy, so I'll stay and—"

Ada interrupted him. "But Samuel's coming over." She really didn't want to share Samuel with her brother. The two men were the same age, and when they got together they always ended up talking about how the Alcott banking empire was doing, or how John enjoyed his doctoring work as a Fellow with the New York Academy of Medicine.

"And why is that a problem?" he asked with a smile.

"You know how you two are. When you get together you always end up talking about banking or doctoring."

"My, my, sister. How greedy you are, wanting Samuel all to yourself. I was merely—"

Nana interrupted. "Leave her alone, Johnny. If you had a sweetheart, you'd want time alone with her."

John acknowledged Nana with a bow. "Touché, Nana. In deference to you—and true love—once Samuel arrives, I'll make myself scarce." He turned to Ada. "When will he be here?"

"Anytime now. He was coming this afternoon to take me to the art museum, but sent word he's eager to see me this morning."

"Eager is good," Nana said. "Very good."

"I like *eager*, too," John said with a grin and made himself comfortable in a chair.

Ada ignored him—which never worked but was her only recourse. She addressed Nana. "I wore my new dress today. I can hardly wait to add scraps from this dress to my bridal quilt. I don't have any aubergine."

"The deep purple will make a lovely addition, I'm sure."

"Absolutely *lovely*," John said, drawing out the word.

The knocker sounded on the front door.

"He's here," Nana said. "Smile prettily."

John showed Ada a toothy grin.

Waiting for Wilson to show him in, Ada started to sit, then stood, knowing the drapery of her new day dress was at its best advantage while she was standing. She had just adjusted the drape of the train when she looked to the foyer and saw Samuel—with a little girl.

Samuel removed his hat and entered the parlor, urging the girl forward. "Good morning, Ada. Mrs. Bauer. And hello there, John. Nice to see you."

Ada was stunned into silence, her focus on the girl. She was seven or eight, and very skinny. She had a cut and horrible bruises on her face, and her coat was threadbare and torn. Ada's heart immediately went out to her. She moved close and put a hand on the girl's head. "Samuel. . .who's this?"

"Her name is Nusa, and last night—"

But before he could answer more fully, the girl tentatively touched the golden trim on Ada's dress. *"Recht,"* she said. *"Sehr recht."*

"She says your dress is very pretty," Nana said. Then she called out to the girl. *"Guten Morgen, liebes Mädchen. Sie sind deutsch?"*

The girl beamed. *"Ja. Sind sie?"*

"Ja!" Nana extended her hands, and Nusa went to Nana's side. The two of them talked back and forth in German.

Samuel moved toward Ada and John. "I didn't know your grandmother knew German."

"She immigrated from Germany when she was young," John said.

Ada couldn't take her eyes off the little girl, chattering on with Nana as if they were already friends. "Nana tried to teach me German, but Mother insisted I learn French instead."

They all watched as Nana patted the foot of the chaise and Nusa sat at her feet. "They're getting along famously," Samuel said.

"So who is she, Samuel?" Ada asked. "Where did she come from?"

"The boys and I were at Five Points last night, and —"

"You weren't slumming it, were you?" John asked.

"I hate to admit, we were."

Ada didn't know what "slumming it" meant, but she did know that Five Points was the most notorious and treacherous area of all New York. "Way down there?" Ada asked. "Isn't that dangerous?"

"It was dangerous for Nusa. I saved her from being beaten by some hoodlum."

If this happened last night, it meant Samuel must have... "You took her home?"

"I couldn't leave her there. The man was vile. He might have killed her."

"I know the type," John said. "I've done some work down there with the Academy, and the poverty, violence, and disease are rampant."

Ada was proud of Samuel, yet to put himself in such a situation... It was then she noticed a cut on his hand. She took hold of it. "You're hurt."

He pulled his hand away. "Just a scratch, and nothing compared to the bruises Nusa has endured."

John stepped forward. "Would you like me to check her out?"

Samuel considered this a moment, then shook his head. "I truly believe her wounds are superficial—this time."

The German conversation paused and Nana said, "She says her parents are dead, and the man who was beating her was the head of a gang of children he recruited to steal for him. She refused and...the rest you know."

"She has no parents?"

Nusa shook her head. *"Eltern. Nein."*

Samuel ran a hand through his hair. "I was going to take her back to Five Points this morning, to wherever she lived."

Nana nodded and asked Nusa a question. *"Wo leben Sie?"*

Nusa shrugged. Then said something that seemed half German and half English.

Nana translated. "She sometimes stays at the Merciful Children Foundling Home. Otherwise, she sleeps on the street."

Nusa walked over to Samuel and took his hand. *"Ich bleibe mit Ihnen. Ja?"*

"She wants to stay with you," Nana said.

John let out a laugh, then stifled it. "It appears she's adopted you, Alcott."

"Are you keeping her, Samuel?" Ada asked. She thought of her childhood clothes, up in the attic. Surely some of them would fit the girl until new ones could be made.

But before she could voice the offer. . .

"Grandfather says she has to go back," Samuel said. "That's where we're heading right now." He looked at Nana. "Please tell her I'd like to give her a home, but Grandfather. . . I just can't. Tell her I'll take her back to the foundling home. I'll see her safely there."

Nana motioned for Nusa to come close again and spoke to her. At first Nusa shook her head, but Nana persisted, and finally Nusa nodded.

"She understands."

Samuel offered her a bittersweet smile, and the girl ran to him, wrapping her arms around his waist. "I hate to send her back there. But I have no choice."

Ada was torn. Although her heart went out to the girl, she said, "Perhaps it *will* be for the best."

Samuel gave her a look that made her immediately regret her comment.

"I mean, she'll be with children of her own kind. . .people who speak German. . ." She looked to John and Nana for help.

"You can't dig yourself out of that one, sister," John said.

Nana chastised him. "Behave yourself, Johnny." To Ada she said, "You may be right, Ada, but being right doesn't equal being fair."

Samuel spoke to Nusa. "Are you ready to go?"

Nusa looked at Nana. *"Gehen?"*

Nana nodded. *"Gehen. Gott segnen Sie und halten Sie, liebes Mädchen."*

Nusa ran to Nana and embraced her. Everything was happening so fast. Samuel was leaving with the girl, taking her back to Five Points. . . .

"Can I come with you?" Ada asked.

Although Samuel looked pleased at her offer, he said, "Another day, Ada."

After they left, Ada sank onto a chair. She ran her fingers along the golden trim that had so impressed the little girl. Golden trim that seemed ridiculously frivolous when compared to the girl's ragged clothes. "I wish he would have let me go with him."

"Five Points is no place for a lady," John said.

"Or a child," she added. "He left so quickly. We have clothes we could give to her, and food. Has she eaten?"

Nana smiled. "I'm sure Samuel has fed her well." Then she beckoned Ada to sit at the foot of the chaise where Nusa had sat just moments before. "You have a good heart, child. As does your Samuel."

"His compassion is one of the reasons I love him."

"You are a good pair, the two of you," Nana said.

Ada nodded. A good pair, who were once again spending time apart.

**

After asking directions multiple times, and getting lost twice, Samuel finally found the Merciful Children Foundling Home. There was a small sign by the front door, but otherwise, the brick building blended into the line of tenements surrounding it. Nusa ran up the steps and opened the door, running inside as if she was truly home.

Samuel was more tentative, not wanting to be the intruder. He stepped inside and called out, "Hello?" He looked down the hall to the left of the staircase and saw a middle-aged woman pull Nusa into an embrace. "Nusa! We're so glad to have you back!"

Samuel was relieved at the warm reception. It would make it easier to leave her behind.

The woman stepped back and took a good look at Nusa's face. "Oh my dear child. How did you get these cuts and bruises?"

"Dieser Mann rettete mich."

The woman looked at Samuel with new appreciation. She walked toward him, extending her hand. "Thank you for saving her. Welcome, Mr. — ?"

Samuel shook her hand. "Samuel Alcott."

"Eliza Hathaway. Please come in, Mr. Alcott."

She led him into a parlor crowded with mismatched chairs, all facing in one direction. It reminded him of a school room. She turned two chairs around. "Please. Sit."

He did so, placing his hat and gloves on his lap. Nusa climbed onto Mrs. Hathaway's lap.

"Well now," the woman said. "Tell me how the two of you met."

Samuel gave the shortened version of their meeting.

"Nusa did not exaggerate. It appears you are a hero," Mrs. Hathaway said.

Samuel shrugged. "I'm just glad she's safely here."

There was a bang overhead, then a stampede of footfalls racing down the stairs. Nearly a dozen children burst into the parlor, ignored him, and ran to Nusa, hugging and exclaiming and loving her back into their presence.

He was moved by their obvious affection for the girl and felt good about his decision to bring her home. Being around people who showed their love overshadowed any *things* he might have been able to provide for her back at his grandfather's house, where Nusa would be alone all day but for the servants.

His presence was no longer needed, so he stood and removed a fold of money he'd prepared as a donation. "I'll be going now. I'm just glad Nusa is safely home. And I want to give you this. . .for the children." Mrs. Hathaway took the money and slipped it into the pocket of her apron. "We are appreciative, Mr. Alcott. But please don't leave so soon. I have soup on the stove and fresh bread in the oven. If the finicky stove behaves itself, it will be a good meal. Please join us. It's the least we can do to thank you."

He didn't want to take their food, which was probably a precious commodity, but when Nusa wiggled her way through the crowd of children and took his hand, he succumbed. "That would be very nice, Mrs. Hathaway. Thank you."

"I may be old, but it's Miss Hathaway, and you can save your thanks for after the meal when you decide whether you like my cooking."

**

The soup was tasty — but secondary to Samuel's dining experience. What fed him more than the meal was the children.

They sat on benches on either side of a huge table in the kitchen, a stairstep of ages and a world of nationalities. They were polite and, for the most part, well mannered. When twelve-year-old Tito sloshed his soup over the side of the bowl, he was quick to say he was sorry, and Miss Hathaway was quick to forgive and help him clean up.

Samuel remembered his own boyhood spills. Grandmother had responded with the same kindness as Miss Hathaway. But

Grandfather had always been quick to jump on Samuel's irresponsibility or rowdiness or clumsiness or rudeness or. . .

He shook the memory away with a shiver. He was still trying to please his grandfather.

With the meal finished, he took a toddler named Kristin to his lap, where she showed interest in his shiny brass buttons. When she smiled at him. . .he'd never felt such a warmth inside.

"You're a natural, Mr. Alcott."

"Excuse me?"

Miss Hathaway nodded at the little girl. "The children love you."

"They're very tolerant."

She shook her head adamantly. "Actually, they're not. Most of them have lived on the streets and are wary of strangers. Because they've fended for themselves, they have acute instincts about people. They know a compassionate man when they see one."

He'd never thought of himself in such a way. As an accountant in his grandfather's bank, he was used to dealing with numbers, facts, and ledgers.

"Don't shake your head no," Miss Hathaway said. "Whether you've had a chance to act on your compassion in the past, you've acted on it now, and once the door's open, there's no turning back."

He didn't know what she was implying.

He must have offered a befuddled expression, for she laughed. "Don't worry, Mr. Alcott. I'm not expecting you to move in and help me or sign over your fortune, but I do know how God got *me* here, and. . .well. . .let's just say I'm looking forward to seeing what happens next."

"Next?" Samuel was confused. One minute he was playing with Kristin, and the next Miss Hathaway was talking about God and opened doors and the future.

Miss Hathaway was still chuckling when she brought him his coat and gloves and placed his hat upon his head. "It's time to go now, Mr. Alcott."

"You're kicking me out?"

"I'm nudging you forward. You have a lot of thinking to do."

He stepped over the bench, placed Kristin on the floor, and put on his coat. "I don't know what you're talking about, Miss Hathaway."

"You don't need to, because I'm not the one who's going to do the talking." She led him to the door. "Good day, Mr. Alcott. Until next time."

He found himself on the street. It was beginning to snow, a soft, cleansing snow that was turning the harsh street into something beautiful.

What had just happened?

He buttoned his coat against the cold, put on his gloves, and walked to an intersection to hail a cab. Once inside, he looked out the window and saw the view of the Merciful Child Foundling Home fall from view.

And then he knew.

He *would* see it again.

He *would* be back.

Chapter Three

"Mr. Alcott? Sir?"

Samuel looked up from his desk to find the head teller standing before him. "Yes, Mr. Taylor?"

Taylor asked him a banking question, and Samuel managed an answer. Not that the question was very difficult, but moving his thoughts from Nusa and the foundling home to banking took some effort.

He could not get the children off his mind.

Or Ada.

Or how the one could ever be connected to the other.

Ada was the woman he was going to marry. She was beautiful, talented, and kind, but was from a class far removed from Nusa's world. She'd offered to accompany him to Five Points, yet the thought of her in such an awful place made him cringe. Ada was innocent of such horrors. She worked with the other ladies of their set making items to sell in philanthropic fund-raising, but that was far different from walking the streets among rats who raced between piles of debris, or smelling the stench of garbage and worse, or seeing — and being seen by — rough men who would not treat her in the way she deserved.

He'd bowed out of their trip to the museum, and to Ada's credit she had not complained. So tonight he would make it up to her. He'd take her to a romantic dinner at Delmonico's. And if everything went as planned, perhaps on Christmas Day he would get down on one knee and propose to her. In fact, he hoped to go shopping at Tiffany's in the next week or so and buy an engagement ring. He'd been saving for months in order to have enough money for a ring that would show her exactly how much he loved her. Although his grandfather was wealthy, Samuel relied on wages and a monthly allowance. He was due to inherit a fortune, but until then Grandfather wanted to "test his mettle," which was fine with Samuel. He enjoyed the satisfaction of earning a living. It was how his grandfather and father had started out, so he was following in their footsteps.

But how much money did he have in his personal account?

Samuel took out his private ledger and looked at the bottom line. He had $212 saved for a ring. Surely that would be enough to buy Ada something beautiful.

He looked up when his grandfather came in his office, and he slid the ledger out of sight. "What can I do for you, Grandfather?"

The older man smiled — which was unlike him. Then he put a small red box on Samuel's desk. "I have a gift for you, or rather a gift for you to pass along. It's been in the safe here at the bank since your grandmother's death and. . ." He pointed to the box. "Open it."

Samuel opened the hinged box and saw a familiar topaz ring. "It's Grandmother's."

"It's her engagement ring. I thought you might want to give it to Ada. If you'd like. It's just a thought."

Samuel had never seen his grandfather so sentimental. And to give up his wife's ring. . .this was monumental.

Samuel removed the ring from the velvet box. It was too small for even his pinky finger, and the gold filigree work around the smoky-colored stone was delicate. "Ada will love it, especially since it was Grandmother's."

"When are you planning to propose?"

Samuel started to say "Christmas," but suddenly felt an inner stirring that stopped him.

"Why the hesitation?" Grandfather asked. "He who hesitates is lost, Samuel. You know that."

Samuel nodded. "I'll propose soon."

"Good. See that you do. Now. . .have you finished wading through the Morrison accounts?"

"Not yet."

"Get to work, then."

And he was gone.

Samuel sat looking at the ring, remembering it on his grandmother's finger. How he wished she were here now to help him deal with his confusion over the pull he felt from the children, and the pull he felt from Ada. "What should I do?" he said aloud. "You always taught me to think of others first, and I want to help the children. But how? I work, I spend time with Ada. . . . How can I help one without slighting the other?"

He put the ring back in its box and set it on top of the ledger.

The ledger.

He opened it and saw the $212 he'd saved for a ring. Now he had a ring. Now he had two hundred and twelve dollars he could spend on something else.

Someone else.

A plan came to mind. Tonight he would talk to Ada about the money and the needs of the foundling home. Together they could come up with a way to spend it.

The children and Ada reconciled, Samuel got back to work.

**

Samuel took a bite of his squab and smiled. "You look ravishing tonight, my love."

Ada felt ravishing. Her apple-green and cream evening dress boasted a heavily embroidered front edged with soutache braid. The short sleeves and side panels of the dress were decorated with rows of tasseled loops of Venetian pearl beads. She wore a rose and white aigrette of ostrich feathers in her hair and carried a matching feather fan. Her neck was adorned with the string of pearls her parents had given her for her coming-out three years ago.

She appreciated his compliment and looked around the restaurant. "I'm glad you got us a table away from the main dining room. I miss having time alone with you."

"And I with you. And since we are alone, I have something I'd like to discuss with you."

Ada's heart added an extra beat. Was he going to propose? The setting was romantic; the evening was going well. Was the moment she'd been waiting for about to become a reality? She set her fork down, wanting her hands to be free when he knelt beside her and placed a ring upon her finger.

She managed to keep her voice even. "What would you like to discuss?"

But instead of pushing his chair back and kneeling before her, he simply moved his plate forward and leaned his forearms on the table. "This afternoon I had some unexpected money come my way, and since it's the Christmas season, I would like to use it to buy the children at the foundling home some presents. And Miss Hathaway mentioned that her stove was finicky, and it *did* look to be on its last legs. I would like—"

Unwittingly Ada put a hand to her chest and gasped.

"Ada? Are you all right?"

All her wishes, dreams, and expectations rushed forward like waves upon a shore, only to pull back, leaving nothing in their wake.

He reached his hand across the table. "Ada, you're worrying me."

It's your own fault, Ada. Why do you do this to yourself? Why do you create amazing romantic scenarios that can never be fulfilled?

She let her hand find its companion in her lap. She gripped them together, hoping to calm herself. "I'm sorry. You mentioned buying a stove?"

He sat back and studied her a moment. "And presents for the children. I thought we could go shopping together and bring them to the foundling home as a couple."

She reined in her disappointment and managed a smile. "That sounds wonderful, Samuel. I'd be happy to help."

She said the words. If only she fully meant them.

Obviously being kind and good was harder work than she thought.

**

Ada checked on Nana before she went to bed. When she saw her grandmother was sleeping, she started to close the door, but Nana called after her.

"Come back, child. I'm awake. I want to hear about your evening."

In the time it took to walk from the bedroom door to Nana's bedside, Ada decided *not* to mention her dashed hopes for a proposal. She didn't want her grandmother to think she was one of those desperate girls who weren't content until they had a ring on their finger.

"Turn up the lamp," Nana said. "I want to see you better."

Ada did as she was told, then perched on the edge of the bed.

"You look beautiful, child. Stunning and. . .and sad. What happened?"

Ada let loose an exasperated sigh. "How do you do that? How do you always see what I really feel?"

Nana patted Ada's hand. "Because I love you so much." She pointed to the water carafe on the bedside table. "My throat is sore. Pour me some water; then tell me what happened."

Ada poured the water, then moved to the bedside chair and told Nana everything: her hopes and expectations, and the reality of Samuel's commitment to the foundling home. "I'm very willing to choose presents with him, even go there to distribute them, for I'd love to check on Nusa. But it *was* a disappointment."

"I thought you said you expected a proposal at Christmas."

"I did, but when he arranged this romantic dinner for two, I just thought — "

"You thought like a woman, like a girl. Do yourself a favor and stop trying to orchestrate events to fit your imagination. Do you truly believe Samuel will propose?"

"Yes."

"Then embrace that certainty and let it happen when it's going to happen."

"You're right, Nana. I know you're right."

"Of course I am." Nana leaned her head back, deeper in the pillows. She closed her eyes.

She was flushed and perspiring.

Ada rose and put a hand to her forehead. "Nana, you're on fire. You have a fever."

"I'm not feeling very good right now, but it will pass."

Ada wasn't going to risk it. She ran to get her brother, the doctor.

Chapter Four

"It's influenza," John said.

During the night Nana's room filled with family as Mother and Father joined Ada in a bedside vigil. At the news, they all took a step back.

"That's contagious, isn't it?" Mother asked.

John nodded. "Yes, it is. And I would guess we've all been infected. I think it would be best if we avoid going out in public, so as not to spread it around."

Ada immediately thought of Samuel. "But I'm going with Samuel to the foundling home to distribute some gifts."

John shook his head vehemently. "Not anymore, you aren't. You don't want to risk infecting those children, do you?"

"But I feel fine."

He gave her a chiding look. "Samuel can survive without you for a few days."

"Days?"

Nana stirred, and Ada went to her. "I'm here, Nana."

"I'm sorry to be so much trouble."

"You're never trouble to me. Ever."

Samuel and the children would have to wait.

**

Samuel paid the clerk $63.25. "Can you have it delivered today?"

The clerk put the money in a money box and made a face.

Since it was clear he was going to say no, Samuel added, "It's for an orphanage. They really need the stove as soon as possible." He handed the man five more dollars. "Will this help?"

The man slipped the fiver into his pocket. "Give me an address, and I'll send George out with it right away."

Samuel wrote down the address, feeling giddy at his accomplishment. He imagined Miss Hathaway's face when the stove arrived.

He wanted to do more than imagine. He wanted to be there. That being the case, he hurried off to Bloomingdale's shoe department to buy shoes for the children. He'd have to guess on sizes, but he hoped if he got an assortment, there would be a pair for everyone.

And some candy. . .when was the last time these children had candy?

The only cloud to the day was that Ada wasn't with him. He'd received her note and understood her need to stay with her grandmother, and her desire not to pose a health risk to the children. He just hoped that *she* would stay well. That said, he still missed her being a part of this special task.

Until next time. For he knew there would be a next time.

**

Money talked. For by the time Samuel finished his shopping and traveled to the foundling home, the new stove had arrived, and the old one was being carted away. Samuel slipped past the delivery men and followed the sounds to the kitchen.

The place was in an uproar, with the children gathered round the new stove, touching its chrome trim, removing its burner covers. As soon as he entered and set down his other gifts, Miss Hathaway saw him. She ran to him, encasing him in a bear hug. "Words cannot express, Mr. Alcott. Words cannot express. . . ."

Not knowing what else to say, he lifted the boxes of shoes, which were tied together with string. "I have something else for each of you."

The children swarmed around him, wanting to know what was in the boxes. Tito, one of the oldest, read the word on a box. "Shoes? Shoes! He brought us shoes!"

Miss Hathaway got scissors to cut the string, and the boxes tumbled to the floor. Samuel stepped back and let the children find shoes that fit.

"Shoes, too, Mr. Alcott?" Miss Hathaway said. "Most of these children have never had new shoes."

"I wasn't sure about size, and I didn't even know their ages. So when the clerk asked me, I had to guess, telling her there were three children this tall, two this tall, all the way down to the baby. I brought fifteen pairs, just to make sure."

The older children helped the younger, and Samuel ended up helping Nusa put on her button shoes. Nusa walked in a circle, trying them out. *"Danke, Herr Alcott!"* She wrapped her arms around Samuel's neck, and at her example, all the other children followed suit.

Their gratitude was embarrassing. Never had there been a better use of his money.

But he had one more surprise. He reached into the inner pocket of his coat and removed sticks of candy. The children's eyes grew big.

"You've outdone yourself," Miss Hathaway said, shaking her head.

It was only the beginning.

**

The children were in the parlor having a lesson given to them by a part-time volunteer named Lottie.

Samuel sat with Miss Hathaway in the kitchen, alone but for the baby, Dolly, who slept in her arms.

"Today I'd hoped to bring along my intended, Ada. But her grandmother—"

"You're engaged?" Miss Hathaway asked.

Samuel avoided the question. "Last night when I took her to dinner at Delmonico's, I asked her—"

"You proposed last night? How romantic. I've never been to Delmonico's, but I've heard how special it is. What a romantic setting for a proposal. It *was* romantic, wasn't it?"

She'd turned the conversation offtrack. "Yes, I suppose it was romantic, but I didn't propose. I asked her if she wanted to come with me to buy a stove and some gifts for the children."

Miss Hathaway stopped rocking the baby. "You're in a fancy restaurant, just the two of you, having a romantic dinner, and you ask her to help you buy a stove?"

She made it sound ridiculous. "Well, yes."

She laughed. "I'm sure she was thrilled with *that* proposal."

Samuel thought back. Ada hadn't been thrilled. In fact, she'd turned a bit quiet. "Do you really think she expected me to propose? I mean, I plan to do so soon, but I hadn't ever thought of asking her last night."

Miss Hathaway shook her head. "If the question looms *soon*, as you say, I'm sure she *had* considered last night could be the night."

Samuel felt like a fool. Poor Ada. She'd hoped for the stars, and he'd given her. . .

A stove.

"There, there now, Mr. Alcott," Miss Hathaway said. "I didn't mean to make you feel bad. Just go over to her house and make amends."

"But I can't. There's sickness in the house. We can't see each other. But I suppose I could send her a note. . . ."

Miss Hathaway chewed on this a moment. "I know something better. Speak to her through flowers. Stop at Thorley's on the way home — isn't that where your set buys their flowers? Have some sent to her house. It's the least you can do."

The very least.

**

"I hate that I've kept you from spending time with Samuel," Nana said as Ada adjusted her pillows.

"Hush now. I'm where I'm supposed to be."

Nana touched her hand. "I do like your company. If only I felt better. . ."

Ada was worried about her grandmother. Because she was already frail, this new illness was dangerous. Even if John had not forbidden Ada from leaving the house, she would have stayed.

Once Nana was settled, Ada returned to her bridal quilt. She'd brought the entire quilt in the room because she was adding three finished quilt blocks to the larger piece.

Nana must have been watching her, for she said, "It's quite a feat, that quilt. A chronicle of your life."

Ada stretched the bulk of the quilt over her lap and stroked it. "It's my life's work."

"Until you marry. Then what will you do?"

"I'll start another quilt, a marriage quilt."

"A family quilt," Nana said. "A big family."

"If you're wanting me to blush, you're going to be disappointed," Ada said. "I agree with you. I want many, many children, and I'll make them each a quilt of their own."

Nana laughed. "You're going to be very busy."

The talk of children made Ada think of Nusa. Was she safe? Had Samuel purchased a stove yet? What else would he buy for them?

"How many blocks do you have left to finish your quilt?" Nana asked.

Ada turned her thoughts back to her work. "I have the scraps from my Christmas dress ready to use in a block commemorating my engagement, which will start the last row that will culminate in a block that will include scraps from my wedding dress."

"You have it all figured out."

The door opened and John entered carrying a bouquet of blue violets. "I come bearing gifts," he said.

"For me?" Nana asked.

"Actually, no. They're for Ada."

She read the note: *I love you. I miss you. And I hope your grandmother gets better soon. . .Samuel.*

"From Samuel?" Nana asked.

She nodded. "But blue violets. . . What's the symbolism?"

"Get the book," Nana said.

John sat at the foot of Nana's bed, shaking his head. "You women and your language of flowers. As if Samuel even knows what blue violets mean."

"Thorley's House of Flowers knows. Just wait. . ." Ada hurried to her room and brought back *The Language of Flowers*, a must for any girl of marriageable age.

She looked under the V section. "Violets — Blue: faithfulness."

"That's lovely," Nana said.

"That's boring," John said.

Ada had to admit she was a bit disappointed in the flower choice. . . If only Samuel had sent her red roses or chrysanthemums, which were symbols of romantic love.

She was being petty. Flowers were flowers.

She wasn't given the chance to discuss it further, as John attended to Nana, his patient.

It was just as well.

Chapter Five

"There," Samuel said, righting the stool with its repaired leg. "Four chairs and a stool, all fixed."

Eliza—for they called each other by their first names now—was at her new stove, stirring a pot of potatoes. "I had no idea you were a carpenter, Samuel."

"Neither did I."

"You like this, don't you?"

"I do enjoy fixing things."

Eliza shook her head. "You like *this*. All of this, working with the children, making them safe and happy."

He sat on the stool to test its stability. Two-year-old Bertie toddled into the room, dragging a blanket behind him, and Samuel took him on his knee. "I do like it. During these past two weeks I've never felt more fulfilled, or of more worth to the world."

"You do have worth here, and I'm not just talking about the new stove, or the shoes, or the new window in the boys' room, or the stack of wood over there."

He was embarrassed by the praise, but it stirred an issue that had been on his mind. "I have worth *here*," he said. "Only here."

"I'm sure that's not true," Eliza said. "Not true at all."

"It feels true."

"In a few days it's Christmas, and you're proposing to Ada. You will find your worth in your new wife and in your new life together."

Instead of affirming Eliza's words, he found himself shaking his head. "I don't know what to do. I love Ada deeply, and until coming here, marriage *was* the next step."

Eliza stopped stirring and took a deep breath, as if needing extra air to fuel her words. "But now your heart has expanded to include. . ." She pointed at little Bertie, who was sticking his fingers through the buttonholes in Samuel's vest.

He nodded.

As did she. Then she sat on the bench facing him. "That's how it happened with me, Samuel. I was the nanny to a wealthy family in England. But when the girl grew too old, I suddenly had a life of my own. And so I came here, to New York City. I met a man on the boat, and during our voyage, we fell in love and began to talk of a life together." She looked at her lap.

"What happened?" Bertie stopped his playing and cuddled against Samuel's chest. Samuel cupped his head with a hand.

"We ended up at Five Points, along with a million other immigrants. Once here, I saw the children in need and knew I had to do something to save them. And so I used what little money I had and rented this place and took them in, trusting God to provide contributions and food and clothing enough to keep us open."

"And the man?"

She shrugged. "He had other plans that did not involve raising other people's children." She retrieved the lap quilt Bertie had dragged into the room and helped Samuel wrap it around the toddler.

"I'm sorry," he said, tucking Bertie in.

"I'm not." She went to check the potatoes. "I sacrificed one kind of love for another." She glanced over her shoulder at him. "Perhaps Miss Wallace could join you in your work here?"

He laughed, then felt guilty for it. His attention was drawn to the quilt around Bertie. He fingered the faded blue cottons. "You should see the bridal quilt Ada's making, full of velvets and satins, embellished with all sorts of embroidery. Not practical at all. She's not practical."

"She's had no reason to be. Perhaps you give her too little credit. If she loves you, she'll join you in your work. For isn't marriage a partnership?"

Samuel remembered that Ada *had* offered to come with him to take Nusa home. He'd been the one to tell her no, because Five Points was no place for a lady.

No place for Ada.

Looking around the room—even though he'd grown fond of this place and enjoyed using his allowance to provide for some of its needs—he had a hard time imagining Ada here. How could he ask a princess to visit a slum?

Eliza stopped her work and looked at him. "Forgive an old woman for stirring things up. You and Ada have your whole lives ahead of you. Relish each other and the time you have together."

"But you gave up your love and your time together."

"What's right for one is not right for all."

And yet. . .

As Samuel rocked little Bertie to sleep, the subject haunted him.

**

Samuel sat at his desk at the bank—a desk that had been vacant too many days as he'd given much of his time to the foundling home. He felt disconnected, as if he was returning to another life.

For that's what it was. In the bank he was Samuel T. Alcott, heir to the Alcott fortune. At the Merciful Children Foundling Home he was Papa Samuel, a colleague, and a member of a family.

And then there was his life with Ada. Because of the influenza, they hadn't seen each other in weeks. They'd communicated through notes, but notes were far from enough.

He felt her slipping away—and knew it was his fault, that he was the one backing up and putting distance between them.

Samuel's grandfather entered his office, his face stern.

"Good morning, Grandfather."

The elder Alcott skipped the pleasantries and pointed a finger toward Samuel's desk. "Get out your personal ledger."

Samuel's stomach flipped. He knew what was going to happen and had dreaded the moment. But there was no escape.

He pulled out the ledger and handed it over. His grandfather opened it, ran a finger along the columns, and jabbed at the final number.

"What's this here? I see you've gone through all your allowance this month—and then some."

"I've had a few expenses of late."

"I never thought Ada was such a demanding girl. After you marry you'll have to put her on a budget."

Samuel hated that Ada had taken the blame. "The money hasn't gone to Ada."

His grandfather hesitated. "You haven't been gambling, have you?"

"Of course not." He might as well say it. "I've been working down at Five Points, at a foundling home. They've needed some repairs and supplies, and I've used my money for that."

Grandfather paused, but only for an instant. "It's that orphan girl you brought home, isn't it? She's the cause of all this."

"She was the impetus that opened my eyes to their need."

"Charity is fine, Samuel—it's even commendable—but there is a limit."

Samuel found the statement odd. "Is there?"

His grandfather's eyebrows rose. "So you wish to give all your money to the poor."

"Isn't that what Jesus told the rich man to do?"

"What are you talking about?"

It was a Bible story his grandmother had taught him, a story forgotten until lately. "A rich man approaches Jesus and asks what he must do to gain eternal life. Jesus tells him he needs to be willing to give up everything, distribute it to the poor, and follow Him."

Grandfather stood there aghast, which made Samuel panic.

"We have so much, Grandfather, and they need so much. In fact, I thought it would be wonderful if we could build them a better place, perhaps in a safer neighborhood, and—"

Grandfather planted a finger on the desk, leaning forward. His voice was a harsh whisper. "*I* have so much. You have nothing without me. And if you continue with this folly, I will make sure you get nothing *from* me. Not a penny."

Samuel couldn't believe what he was hearing. How could his grandfather threaten to disinherit him? How had his simple acts of kindness come to this?

His anger pushed him to standing— but his legs were weak. "Then there it is. We're in agreement. You want to give nothing, and I want to receive nothing." On impulse, Samuel grabbed his coat and hat from the rack.

"Where are you going?"

"To a place where I'm truly needed."

His grandfather's voice softened. "Whoa now, boy. You're needed here, Samuel. And I do admire your altruistic heart. But God also wants us to be wise, and to be strong and do the work."

"But the important work is not here at the bank."

Grandfather shook his head. "There, you are wrong. For without the investment of this bank's money, dozens of businesses would not exist. Hundreds—if not thousands—of people would not be employed in those businesses, and all those families would be hungry and in need. You must find balance, boy. It does not have to be all or nothing. You need to find a compromise."

Samuel knew what his grandfather was saying was wise and prudent. But he was weary of straddling both worlds. "I'm being torn in two. Or three."

"Then mend yourself together again." Grandfather moved to leave the office, then turned one last time. "I don't discount your situation, Samuel, but enough is enough. Your work here, your life here, deserves more than you're giving it."

"Perhaps it's more than I have to give."

Grandfather was taken aback. "What are you saying?"

Samuel wasn't sure — until he heard his own words. "I'm done here, Grandfather. I'm done with this life. I choose to go where I'm truly needed, to the place where God has led me."

"Don't be ridiculous. God's put you right here, and it's time you set aside this other nonsense and get to —"

Samuel felt as if he would burst. "I'm sorry, but I can't. I just can't." He brushed past his grandfather and left the office.

Grandfather called after him. "If you leave this building, you're giving up your job *and* your home. You'll be on your own, Samuel. Completely on your own!"

Samuel's heart beat wildly in his throat as he raced through the bank and out onto the street. He strode down the sidewalk, his head low, his coat flowing behind him. With each step he repeated an admonition. *What have I done? What have I done?*

Then suddenly, he stopped. *I know exactly what I've done. And I know exactly where I need to go.*

He walked on.

Ada poured Nana some tea. "I'm so glad you're feeling well enough to come down to the parlor. I'm sure you're ready for a change of scenery."

"I'm ready to feel well. I'm weaker than a newborn foal."

Ada was not surprised. Nana had eaten little but soup and Carr's crackers for weeks. "What if I ask Cook to make you some toast?"

"With apple butter?"

Ada smiled. "If I have to make it myself." She pulled the bell pull, summoned the maid, and made her request. Then she settled in with her proposal quilt block, readying the scraps of her Christmas dress for application. The red and green plaid was festive and joyful—as she would be on that happy day—just two days away.

They heard someone at the door, and Ada stood, ready to receive their visitor.

Wilson answered it, and Ada was thrilled to see Samuel come in. She rushed into the foyer, ready to encase him in an embrace. It had been so long—too long.

But something about his stance made her hold back.

"I'm sorry to come unannounced," he said, "and I wasn't sure if you were seeing visitors yet, but I. . .I. . ."

His face was drawn, his forehead furrowed. Something was terribly wrong. "I'm glad you came. I've missed you terribly. Please come in. Today Nana has come downstairs for the first time."

After Wilson took his coat and hat, Samuel ran a hand through his hair. Then he followed Ada into the parlor. "Mrs. Bauer. How good to see you up and around."

"How good to be up and around," she said. "Please sit, Samuel, and tell us what's happened in the world during the weeks of my confinement."

He took a seat but seemed baffled by her question. This was not like Samuel, who was always at ease talking about any subject. "I'm afraid I haven't been out in the world much lately, Mrs. Bauer. I've been busy with. . ." He looked to Ada. "Ada, pardon me, but may I speak to you in private, please?"

From the tone of his voice, that was the last thing she wanted, but Nana gave her permission, saying, "Go on now, children. I'm ready to take a little doze. Go have your discussion in the morning room."

Ada kissed her grandmother, then led Samuel to her mother's study. Sunlight streamed through the east windows, warming the room. She closed the doors.

He motioned toward the settee, and she took a place at one end, while he sat at the other. He seemed totally exhausted, and nervous, and. . .

"You're scaring me, Samuel."

"I'm sorry. I don't mean to, but. . ." He took a fresh breath and the words came out in a rush. "My grandfather and I had an argument, and I'm disinherited. I've also lost my job and am not welcome in my home—his home."

Ada had no idea what to say, but finally managed, "Why?"

"Because of the foundling home. I've been spending some of my—most of my— time and money there, repairing things and buying them much-needed supplies, and he doesn't approve. He's cut me off and turned me out."

A thousand thoughts pummeled Ada's mind. She wanted to support him, but he was foolish to alienate his grandfather and lose everything. Surely some compromise could be made. "I appreciate your heart for the poor, Samuel. And I applaud your generosity. But must it be all or nothing?"

He sat silent a moment, his breathing heavy, his eyes locked on the air between them. "I feel called to help them, Ada. It's as if this is what I was born to do. It's my destiny."

Her empathy weakened. "I thought being married to me was your destiny. You've told me as much."

"I know." His eyes met hers, and a wave of panic flowed through her until she felt ready to drown. "I believed that. But I don't know how to reconcile my love for you with this *purpose* I feel compelled to fulfill."

"I thought we were getting engaged. You said you were giving me something special at Christmas. This isn't what I had in mind."

"Nor is it what I had in mind."

She took his hands. "Then don't do it, Samuel. Help the children, but marry me."

He shook his head back and forth, back and forth. "I have no home, no job, and no income. I have nothing to offer you."

She put a hand upon his heart. "Offer me this. I only want your heart, Samuel. You know you already have mine."

He stood, causing her hands to fall away. "I can't marry you, Ada. I can't make you suffer for my choice."

"But I choose you and all that you are, and all that you do." A new thought surfaced. "I'll go with you and help you with your work. We can do it together."

His face turned wistful. "God called *me* to this, Ada. It's not for everyone. It's not for you."

"But how do you know? How do I know? You're not giving me a chance."

He stood. "I have to leave."

"Samuel!"

Ada ran after him, through the wide hallway and into the foyer where Wilson hurriedly gathered Samuel's coat and hat.

"Samuel, you can't do this to me. To us."

"I'm so sorry, Ada. I'm so sorry."

The sound of the closing door echoed in Ada's ears.

"Ada?"

It was Nana. Ada hated that she'd witnessed their parting. As had the butler. Soon the entire household would know of her rejection, her shame. For buried within Samuel's rejection was the fact that he didn't trust her heart or her capabilities.

Ada stumbled into the parlor, not daring to meet Nana's eyes.

"What happened?"

She couldn't talk now. She couldn't explain the unexplainable.

Instead, she gathered the scraps of her Christmas dress — the dress she was going to wear on the day of her proposal — and took them to the hearth.

Where they met a fiery death.

Chapter Six

Nearly a year later

Mother stood next to the desk, watching Ada address an invitation. When Ada was finished, she nudged the envelope to her left, waiting for her mother's approval. "Does this look all right?"

Mother took up the envelope for a better look. "Your *M*'s are a bit compressed for my taste, but it will do. What was our final count?"

"If everyone comes there will be seventy-four."

"Very good," Mother said. "Fewer than fifty and a Christmas ball is a mere dance, and too near to one hundred seems overly grand for the season." Mother returned the envelope to the pile. "Do your very best, Ada. This party is essential to your future."

"How's that?"

Mother gave her a look of frustration. "Because most of your friends are betrothed by now."

By now was a decided dig. And though her mother's mention of betrothals in relation to the upcoming Christmas party might seem odd to the uninformed, Ada knew her mother hoped that a certain Owen Reed would be so overcome by the festivities that he'd propose that very night.

As far as Ada's hopes? They were less detailed and had a lot to do with simply wanting the whole issue of marriage to be *done*.

"Continue on, Ada. I must consult Mrs. Newly regarding the menu."

Whatever. The intricacies of etiquette made Ada weary. This entire Christmas ball had been her mother's idea. It would be a celebration of the season, but more than that, Ada knew Mother wished it to be a way to show New York society that the Wallaces—and especially Ada—had left the unhappiness of last Christmas behind them.

Last Christmas had been a humiliation, as the news of Ada's rejection spread. That Samuel Alcott, heir to the Alcott banking fortune, had shunned Ada *and* his inheritance in order to play do-gooder in the slums, was the topic of conversation through all of last Christmas, well into the 1890 opera season, not to be overshadowed until the death of New York mogul John Jacob Astor III, and the subsequent squabbling of his family over *his* inheritance.

Ada didn't remember much about last Christmas, or the parties and operas that rang in the new year. The few she'd attended, that is. To put it candidly, the Wallace family had been shunned for the social season as punishment for not securing a happy-ever-after ending to her romance. How embarrassing.

Ada had moved through the dark months of ostracism as if asleep, yet without the ability to happily awaken and discover that she and Samuel were still the loves of each other's lives.

She'd only received one note from him over the past year—an apology note. As if a few words could mend the tear in her heart. There had been no return address, and no clue as to the exact location or name of the foundling home. Ada remembered Nusa telling Nana the name of it, but neither one of them could retrieve the exact memory.

In an effort to find him, Ada had even contacted Samuel's grandfather, hoping that he had more information. But Mr. Alcott was also in the dark. Samuel had vanished into the bowels of New York City, unbound and unfound.

In her desperation, Ada had even begged John to help her find him. But John had refused, saying what was done was done. And what would Ada do if she found him? Samuel had broken ties with *her*. And even if he had changed his mind, was Ada willing to give up the life she knew for some bizarre life *he'd* chosen?

She'd told herself yes, she was willing. But Ada also knew that words were cheap and the price of a wrong choice was costly. And so her sorrow, which had turned to desperation, evolved into anger. For even after a healthy dose of self-analysis, she couldn't think of a single thing she'd done to cause the drastic change in Samuel. The fact he'd chosen to exclude her from his decision was unfair. He'd never given her a chance. She had no idea if she would have risen to the challenge, but to be denied the opportunity. . .

None of it made sense.

Until the breakup, Ada felt as if God had brought them together. But if that were true, then why had He allowed them to be split apart? Her inability to rectify this question caused her faith to suffer and made her doubt her own inner compass for what was genuine and what was false.

Until Owen Reed came into her life.

Owen had saved her from drowning in a sea of emotion. He was a member of their set and was gentle and kind. It didn't really matter that he was on the shortish side, or that he was an ember to Samuel's fire. That Owen was content with quiet conversations about music or the arts or his latest book of interest was a blessing. He didn't require much effort on Ada's part.

Ada found it appropriate that Owen had saved her at Easter—redeemed her. He'd accosted her after Easter service, and his attention had opened a door, allowing Ada readmittance into New York society.

Her sentence was commuted, and Owen did everything society proclaimed a beau should do. He was her companion to any event she desired to attend, was an able dancer, was conscious of her needs, whether it be getting her a glass of punch the moment she was thirsty or offering her his arm as they negotiated the marble stairs at the opera. He gave and she took, and though she recognized the disparity in their relationship, she was relieved that he seemed content in it.

As was she. As much as she could be.

For with Samuel's departure from her life, so had gone Ada's passion. Not only the physical passion, but also her desire for living, for enjoying the moment, and for thinking of the future with anticipation. Though Owen's presence smoothed over the rawness of her pain, it still hid just below the surface, making Ada fear that feeling too much one way or the other might set it free.

Ada's parents wanted Owen to be the *one*. They appreciated how he *had* been the one to finally break her out of her haze. And above all, his attention saved Ada's mother from a fate worse than death and allowed the Wallace family to step free of their societal banishment. His family was suitable—being *the* Reeds of the Reed shipping fortune. But so far at least, Ada had felt no spark in his presence, no inner tug indicating he was God's choice, just for her.

Nana was the only one who understood the limbo she was in, the uncertainty, and the confusion that assaulted her each morning and clung to her dreams each night.

Ada was surprised to see that she'd completed a dozen more envelopes without conscious thought. If only she could complete all tasks in such a way.

"Psst!"

She looked to the doorway of the morning room and saw her brother.

"How would you like to go shopping?" John asked.

She was surprised that the idea *did* pique her interest. But then she looked back to the invitations. "I'd better not. Mother wants to mail these tomorrow. She's obsessed with this party. It's going to change my life, you know."

He plucked an envelope from the pile. "Your *M*'s are too broad."

She snatched it back from him. "What do you need to buy?"

"Mother says all my gloves are a disgrace, and she will not let me ask a single girl to dance at the ball until I rectify the matter. I am therefore off to Macy's, and was thinking that surely you need some new gloves, a bit of lace, or perhaps some other bit of feminine fluffery?"

She loved how he made her smile. "I suppose I could think of something I need."

He clapped his hands. "Then get your bonnet and cape and let's be off. McCoy is bringing the carriage around."

Shopping. Why not?

**

The carriage stopped with a jerk, causing Ada to lurch forward toward her brother. John took her hands, helping to set her aright.

"Sorry," Ada said.

"I wonder what's going on." John reached behind his head and opened the sliding window in order to speak to the driver. "Careful there, McCoy. We nearly ended up in each other's laps."

"I apologize, Dr. Wallace. But there seems to be some commotion ahead. All traffic is stopped."

"Can you see what it is?"

"Not yet, sir."

Ada knew they were still a long way from Macy's. The sidewalks were busy with people walking hurriedly amid the December cold, their shoulders raised toward their ears, the distance between couples testing propriety as they sought each other's warmth while they braved the weather to travel from here to there. The path of each person was marked by the puffs of their breath.

McCoy tapped on the window. "Excuse me, sir, but there appears to be an accident of some sort in the next block. No one's moving. I'm sorry. There's not much I can do but wait."

Waiting was not Ada's strong suit. She looked out both sides of the carriage to make her own assessment of the situation. *Actually, there – what if we went. . . ?*

"How about there," she said, pointing to a street to their left. "Could McCoy go around the carriage in front of us, turn onto that street, and find a different way?"

John did his own looking, agreed, then told McCoy the plan.

By cajoling the horses and getting the hack in front of him to move up just a bit, McCoy maneuvered their carriage onto a side street.

"I knew it would work," Ada said.

But as they tried to go around the block, various obstructions forced them to continue farther south and east, into neighborhoods that seemed foreign — not just in their unfamiliarity, but in their ethnic roots. Ada saw bearded men with ringlets on each side of their faces, wearing long black coats and flat-topped hats, and signage on shops that was written with an alphabet far beyond the ABCs.

"Well now," John said. "We've wandered into the Jewish area of town. We're way off course."

Ada knew her father had business dealings with Jewish people, and Arthur Wyndym had even bought his fiancée a diamond from a jeweler in this area. But Ada didn't think she'd ever seen a Jewish person.

A little boy ran to catch up with his father, taking his hand. He, too, had the long ringlets. *Jesus was a Jew. . . .*

Had Jesus looked like these men?

But as the carriage moved south, the neighborhood changed as if they had traveled from one country to the next. The buildings were similar, but even in the cold, these had laundry hanging on lines strung between windows. The people were dressed in earthen tones, their hair dark and silky, and their skin slightly darker, as if tanned by the sun. Only there was little sun here. The streets were bathed in shadow, with only a slice of sky showing above. The going was narrow as the street was occupied with a myriad of pushcarts, each with a vocal owner lauding their wares. Bread, apples, baskets. . .

"Pane, pane fresco!"

"Mele deliziose!"

"Bei cestini!"

"You were curious about Five Points, sister? Take a look."

Ada looked around with new eyes. "Samuel lives here. . . ."

"Well, yes, technically, I guess he does, but—"

Suddenly Ada felt an overwhelming need to find him, to be out of the carriage, to look for him, and to see what he saw every day. Since they were stopped, she opened the carriage door. "I'm getting out."

"You can't do that. Ada. . ."

Ada ignored her brother's words and his touch and stepped onto the street.

McCoy called down to her. "Miss Wallace! Please. You must get back in the carriage."

She scanned the crowd, desperately looking for the one face that was always in her thoughts. *Samuel! Please, God. Let me find Samuel.*

But as she stepped away from the carriage, she was overrun with children, their faces grimy and pitiful, their hands outstretched, pulling at her arms and her skirt.

"Signora graziosa. Per favore. Aiuto."

"Una moneta?"

Some held up a piece of paper or chunk of wood, as if trying to sell it to her.

"Compri la mia carta."

"Compri questa parte di legno."

One held up a piece of coal. "Coal, lady? Keep you warm?"

She was appalled yet moved. Were these Samuel's charges? She wanted to push them away even as she wanted to hold them close to comfort them. Their dark eyes were so beautiful, their grimy angelic faces pulled with pleading.

"I'm sorry. I don't have any money."

John appeared at her side, offering them a few coins. "Get on with you now. Away! Shoo! Leave her alone!"

They ran off, scattering in the crowded street and around the pushcarts.

The congestion on the street had become an issue. A horse and cart coming toward them couldn't go any farther. The driver yelled at McCoy in Italian.

"In the carriage, Miss Wallace. Dr. Wallace. I must insist."

"Come now, Ada," John said. "We must get back inside."

With a glance, Ada knew they were right. Commotion swirled around her. The chance to find Samuel was tinged with the menace of the unknown. Ada returned to the carriage and John started to help her inside. She was just raising her skirt in order to negotiate the step when. . .

The driver of the cart yelled at McCoy even louder, his hands gesturing wildly.

McCoy yelled back, and in the ruckus the horses lurched forward. Ada let out a yelp as she lost her footing, stumbled, and fell to the ground.

John rushed to help her up, but the horses. . .and the carriage. . .and the cart. Pushcarts, people, running children, and —

Just as Ada regained her footing, she saw the cart's horse panic and rear up.

She spotted the coal boy in harm's way and yelled, "The boy!"

Ada saw a flash of blue as a man burst out of the crowd and shoved the boy to safety.

The horse came down on the man.

There was an awful thud of hooves against flesh.

Screams.

"Inside!" McCoy demanded, his manners gone. "Now! We must back up and —"

But Ada didn't move. Mesmerized, she watched as a swell of people rushed to the man's aid. In the back of her mind was the accusation: *I caused all this.*

"Ada!" John said. "Get in the carriage. I'm going to help."

She was tempted. For inside the carriage she could hide away and pretend none of this had happened. She could draw the curtains on the windows and close her eyes and wait until McCoy got them to safety.

But the memory of the little boy's eyes assailed her, and the sound of a man being hurt. Added was the knowledge that good medical care was probably a rarity in such a neighborhood.

There was only one thing to do.

She pushed through the crowd until she saw her brother. "John! John! Bring the man to the carriage. Take him away from here."

John looked up from his work on the man, his face a mixture of surprise, diligence, and questions. Then he nodded. "Men, help me. *Aiutilo!*" He pointed to the carriage. "To the carriage. *Veicolo!*"

Enough men understood to do as he asked. Ada rushed back, leading the way. The men got the hero into the carriage, where he fell upon the free seat, unconscious.

John rushed in last. He banged on the side of the carriage. "Go, McCoy. Get us home!"

Somehow, by the grace of God, a path opened and the carriage moved.

John knelt beside the man, pressing a bloody handkerchief to his face.

"Will he be all right?" she asked.

John looked up at her, hesitated, then said, "Ada. . .it's Samuel. Samuel Alcott."

What? She nudged John to the side in order to see the man's face.

"Samuel!"

Samuel opened his eyes for but a moment and whispered one word.

"Ada?"

"Oh, Samuel! I'm so glad we found you. I—"

But Samuel closed his eyes, and his head fell to one side.

Ada's heart stopped. "No! John. . .no. He's not dead, is he?"

John put his fingers to Samuel's neck, then shook his head. "He's alive, but barely so. He saved the boy, but the horse came down on him."

Ada's head shook *no, no, no*. She couldn't lose him now. "Faster, McCoy! Faster!" she yelled.

And then she prayed.

Chapter Seven

Once home, John was no longer Ada's brother, but became Dr. Wallace. He gave orders to the servants and directed Samuel to be taken upstairs to a guest room. Their mother met the commotion with a hundred questions, which John dismissed, his attention wholly on his patient.

Then John asked Ada, "I need help, but I can't have you go squeamish on me. Are you up to it?"

Was she? Helping Nana when she was sick and helping John attend an injured man were far different.

"Well? I need to know."

"Yes, yes, I'll help." *Of course I'll help. It's Samuel.*

"Then get in here."

**

Ada did not have time to feel squeamish or to think about the fact that Samuel was in their house. In the need of the moment he became a generic man in trouble. She surprised herself by being able to separate her emotions from the work, assisting John as he cleaned the open wounds and tried to determine the extent of the deeper injuries.

"He has multiple bruises and contusions, but I don't see any broken bones," John said.

Ada moved to the far side of the bed and helped wrap a bandage around Samuel's arm, keeping the fabric flat and smooth.

"Gentle now," John said.

Only after they were finished did Ada allow her gaze to fall upon Samuel's face. With the blood cleaned away, and his hair swept back. . .

He'd lost weight, but he was still her Samuel. His high cheekbones, his strong brow. She put a hand on his forehead. "Samuel," she whispered, "I'm here."

John cleaned up his instruments and put them in his doctor bag. "I doubt he can hear you. He has a concussion—a blow to the head. As you've seen, he fades in and out of consciousness and is very disoriented. He doesn't understand where he is, and he's delirious."

"Will he be all right?"

"The cuts and bruises will heal, but his internal injuries are unknown."

Ada wanted to place her hands on his wounds and will him to health. She pulled a chair close to the bed. "I'll sit with him."

John put a hand on her shoulder. "You did very well, sister. I didn't know you had it in you."

"Nor did I. I'm just glad I could help."

John looked at her, then at Samuel, then at Ada again. "But please remember this. Just because you found Samuel doesn't mean he's yours again. He left you. He's made no effort to contact you. He's moved on and so have you."

His directness surprised her. "I know."

And she did know. But. . .she couldn't deny that his presence seemed an answer to prayer.

Chapter Eight

The next day Mother appeared in the doorway of Samuel's room and summoned Ada away from his bedside into the hall. "You heard John's orders that Samuel must stay here with us for a while?"

"Is that all right with you, Mother?"

Her gaze strayed toward the bed where Samuel lay motionless. "It's obviously a complication."

That was not a word Ada would choose. "Helping someone in need is not a complication. Would you rather we left Samuel injured on the street?"

"Don't get huffy with me, daughter. I'm simply stating the obvious, that with you on the cusp of being engaged to Owen, the sudden presence of your old beau is awkward."

She was right, of course, and that *rightness* annoyed Ada. "Be that as it may, I'm willing to deal with the awkwardness in order to do the right thing. Owen is a kind man. He'll understand."

"Are you sure?"

"Absolutely," Ada said, though she was *not* sure. Owen was a dear, but would he be put off by the situation?

Yet why would it be a problem? Samuel had spurned her, humiliated her by choosing his calling over her love and by not trusting her to be a part of it. No one understood how he could choose poverty over a privileged life. She also assumed that most people thought he left her because she simply wasn't enough for him. But now. . .the Wallaces had chosen to help the man who'd wounded her so badly, and were doctoring him and nursing him back to health. . . . Wouldn't that cause her society friends to look at her family with respect? Wasn't it proof they'd risen above the pain?

It wasn't as if she was still in love with him.

**

In spite of her protests, Mother insisted Ada go with Owen to Carrie Astor's party that evening. On the carriage ride there, she considered telling Owen about Samuel, but since he was in such a jolly mood—talking about a new shipment his family's business had received from China—she'd been content to let him ramble on.

Once in the midst of the party, she decided a group announcement might be the easiest. She *did* have to say something, for if word got out otherwise—and servants *did* talk—the gossip would be far worse than the reality.

And so, after they'd taken turns playing the piano and entertaining each other with witticisms and song, she told a small group of her friends. "I had an exciting day yesterday."

"Do tell," Carrie said. "For lately, the most exciting thing to happen to me was finding a blue ribbon I thought I'd lost."

Ada scanned the faces of the group, ending with Owen, standing beside her. She told them of her shopping expedition gone awry—leaving out Samuel's identity. For now.

"So you have that man at your house? Sleeping in one of your beds?"

"The accident *was* partially my fault," she explained. "John and I couldn't very well leave him on the street."

David Gould shook his head. "Five Points, you say? I wouldn't let my worst enemy visit that area."

Because Samuel lived there, she downplayed its worst qualities. "It's run-down, for certain, but there were a lot of people selling their wares in pushcarts, and—"

Maribelle Morgan made a face. "You didn't buy anything from them, did you? I mean, who would want to touch such things?"

"No, I didn't get around to buying anything." She thought of the children who'd swarmed around her. "I will admit it was sad to see the children trying to earn a few pennies by selling scraps of coal or wood. They were so desperate."

"Where are their parents?" Carrie asked. "And shouldn't they be in school?"

"I'm not sure they have parents," Ada said. "Or a school to go to."

Thomas Fairfield removed a piece of lint from his trousers and let it fall to its death on the carpet. "Then they should get jobs. The garment industry employs children. Let them earn their keep." He dismissed the subject of the children with a flip of his hand. "Enough of them. When can you be rid of the man?"

Ada hated their attitude. Surely they wouldn't have left an injured man on the street.

"I think it's marvelous you took him in," Owen said, with a hand on her arm. "We are to give generously to the poor and help the helpless. You and John are Good Samaritans."

Maribelle wasn't satisfied. "But a stranger in your house. . ."

It was time for the whole truth. "Actually. . .the man is not a stranger."

Oscar laughed. "*You* know someone in Five Points?"

"I know Samuel Alcott." She turned to Owen, offering him her full attention. "Samuel is recuperating in our house."

It took them a moment to react. "The man who was hurt is Samuel? Your Samuel?" Carrie asked.

Owen's eyes locked on Ada's, obviously needing reassurance. "But he's not her Samuel anymore."

"No, he's not," she told him quietly.

"No, of course he's not," Carrie said. "Silly me. But it *is* Samuel?"

"One and the same." She was glad to break her gaze with Owen. He *did* care that it was Samuel. Oh dear.

Maribelle fanned herself, as if wanting the whole notion to flutter far, far away. "But Samuel hurt you so horribly, Ada. How can you bring him into your home?"

The respect she'd yearned for was obviously not going to be offered.

"How the mighty have fallen," David said, shaking his head.

"He hasn't fallen," Ada said. "Samuel is a good man who simply chose a way of life that's beyond our understanding."

"But he hurt you," Carrie said. "Surely you haven't forgiven him?"

Ada felt her heart start to race. Had she forgiven him?

Her own doubt caused her ire to rise even more. "Instead of focusing on the past, I thought you'd focus on the present, on the needs of a friend. I guess I was mistaken."

"Come now, Ada," Thomas said. "You must admit the entire situation is rather odd and a bit. . ."

"Scandalous," Maribelle said. When no one responded, she scanned the group, ending with Thomas. "Don't look at me like that. Isn't that what you were going to say?"

"I was going to say 'unfortunate.'"

Maribelle's fan fluttered furiously. "My statement stands. Not that Samuel Alcott would care whether he caused a scandal or not. He's already shown a total disregard for society and propriety by abandoning his birthright, disregarding his grandfather's wishes, and breaking the heart of my friend. What goes around comes around."

Ada was fuming inside. "Are you implying he deserved to get hurt?"

Maribelle reddened. "I. . .I'm just saying he put himself in that horrible neighborhood, so what did he expect?"

"He did not expect my family's carriage to detour onto a busy street and cause congestion, upheaval, and injury." She handed her champagne glass to a nearby footman. "Now, if you'll excuse me, I need to go home to see if there is some way I can repair the damage I've caused."

With that, she moved to the front door with Owen rushing after her.

**

"I'm sorry for cutting our evening short," Ada told Owen when they were in the carriage.

"No apologies necessary. But in our friends' defense. . .they were simply surprised at your news." He paused a moment, then added, "As was I."

She took his gloved hand in hers. "I should have told you in private. Forgive me."

He shrugged. "So what does Samuel have to say for himself? Where has he been this past year? What has he been doing?"

"I don't know. We haven't spoken. He's sleeping most of the time, and when he awakens, he's delirious."

"Oh. That's too bad."

But by the tone of Owen's voice, Ada could tell he was relieved.

**

Once home, Ada went to Samuel's room, knocked gently, and, receiving no answer, went inside. The lamp was still burning beside the bed, and John was asleep in a chair.

She stood over Samuel and watched his chest rise and fall. If only he would awaken and know her.

But what would she say to him? How would she greet him?

As a friend?

Or. . .as something more?

She kissed her fingers and pressed them to his hair, leaving the answer to another day.

Chapter Nine

"But why doesn't he know us?" Ada asked her brother.

Nana stood beside her and nodded, making it her question, too.

John took hold of Samuel's wrist, then looked at his pocket watch.

Ada remained quiet while John checked his pulse.

His mission complete, he set Samuel's hand on the covers. "His heart rate is strong, and it's good he *is* waking on occasion and is cognizant enough to take broth and medicine and tend to other functions." He nodded at the footman Patrick, who helped with Samuel's more personal needs. "His realization of where he is and who we are will come."

"What can we do to help?" Ada asked.

He nodded toward the door. "I'll ask a maid to sit with him when either you or I can't be here, but —"

Nana raised a hand. "I can sit with him, too."

Nana rarely got out of bed, and if she did, *she* was the one attended.

"Well, I can," she said. "I can sit in here just as well as I can sit in my room. I always liked Samuel. Let me help."

Moved by her offer, Ada kissed her cheek.

"Your help is accepted," John said. "But I'd feel better if he has a real nurse on hand full-time. At least for these first critical days."

Critical days. Ada didn't like the sound of that. She'd fully expected Samuel to awaken and know her, and be pleased to see her. Was there a chance that he'd never be completely with them?

Nana must have sensed her fear, for she took her hand. "And to do our part, we will increase the intensity of our prayers for his full recovery."

Tenfold. One hundredfold. "Can you arrange for a nurse?" Ada asked.

"I can and will. But I'm sure it will be afternoon before one can come. Can you handle it until then?"

"Of course."

"Me, too," Nana said.

John kissed his grandmother on her other cheek. "You are a constant surprise, Nana. I've never seen you so strong."

"Perhaps the presence of someone who needs more help than myself has been the shoe to boot me out of bed."

Mother came in as John was leaving and they exchanged pleasantries. Then she joined Nana and Ada bedside, though she kept her distance as though Samuel were contagious.

"I hear John's sending over a nurse," Mother said. "Your father will not appreciate the expense."

Nana threw up her hands. "Gracious sakes, daughter, if Horace won't pay the money, I will. Sometimes you two act as cheap as a chicken."

"Shouldn't you be back in your own bed, Mother?"

Nana firmed her grip on Ada's hand. "I'm doing fine right here, thank you."

Then Ada brought up something that had been on her mind. "I wish we could contact the foundling home where Samuel's been living, to tell them where he is—that he's being cared for."

"Do you really think that's necessary?" Mother said.

"Winifred Grace!" Nana said. "Not only are your purse strings tied in a knot, but your heartstrings, too? Think of those worrying. They need to know what's happened."

Even though Ada appreciated Nana's defense, she intervened on her mother's behalf. "I wish we could contact them, but I don't know the name of the home. Samuel only sent the one letter and didn't say."

"He probably didn't want to be found," Mother said. "So that's that, then."

Ada had another task to suggest. "This afternoon I plan to go to Mr. Alcott's to tell him Samuel is here, and he's hurt — before he hears it from someone else." She thought of Carrie Astor, David, Maribelle, and all the rest at the party last night. The speed of the society gossip mill was unparalleled — especially when bad news was involved.

Mother turned up her nose. "*If* Alcott's even around anymore. I haven't heard hide nor hair of him since Samuel ruined his life."

Ada closed her eyes against her mother's barbs. "I must try. You'd want to know if I was hurt, wouldn't you?"

"Don't be silly." Mother turned to leave. "John said you volunteered to sit with Samuel until the nurse arrives?"

"I did."

She nodded, then said, "Perhaps you should get out your bridal quilt and work on it again. It's been a year, Ada. You've always called it a map of your life. You must catch up and create the squares to commemorate your happy times with Owen."

Ada had not even allowed herself to look at the quilt since she'd put it away on the evening Samuel left her. Adding any new square with fabrics and embroidery symbolizing her relationship with Owen would force her to create and stitch a new route to her life's map—one that detoured and traveled down roads she hadn't fully accepted. And if she allowed herself to be honest, roads she wasn't sure she wanted to travel.

She shook her head. "When I'm here I want to give Samuel my full attention."

Mother was persistent. "But when you and Owen become engaged, don't you want to take the quilt into your marriage as you planned?"

Nothing was as she'd planned. "Mother, I said no."

Mother shuffled her shoulders. "It was just a suggestion. The quilt is your prized possession, and it doesn't seem right you've abandoned it because of a little heartache. Things are finally back to normal. Life goes on."

A little heartache? Life goes on? It wasn't that simple. Surely Mother knew it wasn't that simple.

To avoid an argument, Ada moved toward the door. "I think it's best if Samuel rests in silence right now. If you don't mind."

Mother walked into the hallway but offered one last barb. "Watch yourself, Ada."

It took all of Ada's restraint not to slam the door. "Argghhh!"

"Now, now," Nana said. "As much as my daughter and I don't agree, she does have a point about the quilt—your life quilt. In spite of what you believe, your life did not end when Samuel left."

There it was again: *Life goes on.*

Nana slipped her hand around Ada's arm. "Besides, he's back, isn't he?"

"What do you mean by that?"

But Nana only put a finger to her lips and smiled.

**

Ada sent a note to Samuel's grandfather, asking if she might visit him that evening after he got home from work. Soon after the hired nurse arrived, she received word she should come at three. The early hour surprised her, but she was also grateful, for it would prevent her from being out after dark.

A gentle snow was falling—a Christmas snow as Ada liked to call it, for it fell gently, as if covering the city in a heavenly mantle.

The Alcott butler greeted her and took her coat and bonnet, the snowflakes already melted on the warm fabric. "Nice to see you again, Miss Wallace," Briggs said. "We've missed you."

How very kind of him. "I've missed you, too, Briggs. Is Mr. Alcott ready to see me?"

There was a moment of hesitation, and Briggs looked nervously to the floor.

"What's wrong?"

"He's much changed, miss."

"How so?"

"You'll see." The butler led her back to a room she had never entered. "He's in there, miss. He's always in there." Briggs knocked, then opened the door and let her in, closing it behind her.

The room was a study with dark paneling and floor-to-ceiling shelves filled with books. A fire was in the grate, but other than its light and two gas wall sconces turned low, the room was dark. It smelled of lemon oil, leather—and grief.

Ada looked toward the massive desk, expecting to find Mr. Alcott there. But the desk chair was empty. Perhaps he was going to join her in a few minutes. She moved to wait in one of the chairs facing the fireplace, but pulled up short when she saw one was occupied.

"Oh. Sir. Mr. Alcott. I didn't see you there."

He didn't rise, but looked up at her over his spectacles. "That's because I'm not here. Not anywhere." He pointed to the other chair, but it seemed the effort to raise his arm was nearly too much. "There. Sit there."

She sat in the other wing chair, adjusting her bustle against the cushions. "I'm so glad you agreed to see me," she said. "And that you were home from work so the meeting could be early."

He snickered. "Work. What does work matter? What does anything matter without my grandson?"

Ada sucked in a breath. Briggs was right. Mr. Alcott had changed much. Gone was the vibrant—if not domineering—man who ran a banking empire as well as his grandson's life. In his place was this lump of a man with tousled hair, an unruly beard, and rumpled clothes.

She spotted a pillow and blanket on the couch nearby. Was he sleeping in here, too? Had this room become his world?

He looked at her with rheumy eyes. "I always liked you, Ada. I wanted you as my granddaughter, I really did. Since Emma died. . .this family needs a woman's touch."

"Thank you, sir. I wanted to be a part of this family."

"Until Samuel rejected you. And rejected me," he said. "All my life's work was not enough for him. And what is any of it worth without him? When I lost my son in the fire, Samuel became my everything. I may not have shown it well, but that truth remains. And I never thought he'd turn his back on all this—on me. I didn't mean it when I gave him the ultimatum." His voice cracked with emotion. "I didn't mean it."

Her heart went out to him. To feel like such a failure. *Please, God, give me the right words to help him.* Ada reached out to touch his knee. "Mr. Alcott, Samuel's choice had nothing to do with your life's work, or your success, or the legacy you worked so hard to build."

"Then why?"

She searched for a mingling of truth and discretion. "Samuel has a heart unlike any other. He sees when others look away; he feels what others wish to ignore. God called him to do special work, work that demanded sacrifice. You and I are a part of that sacrifice." She took a cleansing breath, then continued. "I, for one, don't like that role. And sometimes I sit and think and pray that I would hear such a call. Yet I fear that even if God called, I wouldn't have the strength to go. Samuel had that strength."

"But he left us behind."

Ada realized that in answering the question for Mr. Alcott, she had answered an unasked question in herself. She fumbled in her pocket for a handkerchief. "I'm sorry. As you see, it still affects me, too."

He plucked his own handkerchief from a pocket, removed his spectacles, and dabbed at his eyes. "We are quite a pair, Miss Wallace, for we have both lost our Samuel."

Suddenly Ada remembered why she had come. "But he's not lost, Mr. Alcott. I found him. And he's at our house."

She filled in the blanks, telling him the complete story.

His eyes cleared, and his face became animated. When she was finished, he surprised her by rising to his feet. "We must go. Now! I must see Samuel!" He hobbled to the door and thrust it open. "Briggs! Come help me. I have to go out!"

**

Samuel's grandfather entered the Wallace household like a hurricane. Not two steps into the foyer, he called out, "Where's Samuel? Where's my grandson?"

Mother rushed out from the parlor, her hand to her chest, clearly concerned about the barbarian who'd invaded her house.

Ada didn't know who to calm first. She chose Mr. Alcott, because it was clear he was unrestrainable. She led him up the stairs, calling down to her mother. "Forgive him. He's just excited."

Mother fumbled some reply, which thankfully Ada couldn't hear.

"Down this way, Mr. Alcott."

But before he could fling the door to Samuel's room open, Ada barred the door. "Now stop. You must contain yourself."

The old man's breathing was labored from the stairs and his zeal. He put a hand to his chest and forced himself to calm down.

"That's better," Ada said.

He nodded, and when he'd fully gotten himself under control, he took Ada's hand and kissed it. "How can I ever thank you, dear girl?"

Get Samuel to fully awaken.

"Are you ready?" she asked.

"I am."

She opened the door. The hired nurse stood near the door, clearly alerted to the uproar outside. Ada tried to reassure her. "This is Mr. Alcott's grandfather. He's very eager to see him."

The nurse raised an eyebrow. "There will be no agitation, no dramatics. Is that understood?"

Mr. Alcott lifted his right hand as if taking an oath.

"Very well then." The nurse stepped aside.

Ada let Mr. Alcott proceed to the bedside alone. She whispered to the nurse, "Any change?"

"None."

Ada had warned Mr. Alcott of Samuel's condition, but seeing his grandson immobile and bandaged... He put a hand to his mouth, and Ada heard a moan escape.

She moved to his side to provide support. "See?" she said, trying to sound positive. "He's really here."

Mr. Alcott nodded, and Ada heard him sniff. He was crying.

She linked her arm through his, and together they watched Samuel sleep.

**

Ada left Mr. Alcott sitting at Samuel's bedside and headed to her room to change from her suit to a day dress.

Passing Nana's room, she heard all sorts of commotion inside. She let herself in.

Nana was sitting at her dressing table. Two maids fluttered around her, one doing her hair and another brushing off a dress.

"What's going on?" Ada asked.

Nana turned around on the bench. "Shame on you for not telling me we have a guest, Ada."

Ada was confused. "You mean Mr. Alcott?"

"Of course I mean Mr. Alcott. Who could help but hear him?" She pointed at the burgundy moire dress. "Do you think this will be appropriate for dinner?"

"Dinner?" Nana had not joined the family for dinner in years.

"I assume he's staying for dinner."

Ada had lost all track of time. It was nearly the dinner hour. "I suppose he could. I haven't asked him."

"Where are your manners, child? Go invite him to stay, and leave me to my toilette."

Ada met the eyes of the maids, and they both shrugged as if they didn't know any more than she did.

There was a story behind all this. . . .

**

There had been much scrambling behind the scenes to set two extra places for dinner and alert the kitchen of the additional guests, not for the quantity — there was always enough food — but for their identity. The invalid Mrs. Bauer had actually dressed for dinner, and the other diner was the grandfather of the injured man upstairs — who used to be Miss Ada's beau. . . . The servants' grapevine would lose its leaves tonight.

Ada saw her grandmother walk into the dining room on the arm of Mr. Alcott. "Look at her," she whispered to her brother.

"Look at them," John said.

They were seated and the dinner service began. Mother looked peeved, but Ada's father was positively jolly. "My, my, Nathaniel Alcott, how good to see you. And Mother Bauer. . .you light up the room."

"Why, thank you," Nana said.

Mr. Alcott smiled at Nana. "The last time I saw you look so lovely was the first of August, 1832."

Nana blushed—she actually blushed! Ada had never seen pink on her cheeks.

And they knew each other?

"It was a Wednesday, Nate. And if I remember correctly—which I do—you looked quite dashing yourself."

Mother's soup spoon clattered onto the table. "Mother! You're a married woman."

"I'm a widow, and Nathaniel is a widower. And in 1832 neither one of us was married."

Mr. Alcott laughed. "We weren't married, and we didn't have more than a nickel in our pockets. We'd just arrived in New York City."

"We met on the voyage over," Nana said. "Nathaniel and I had quite the shipboard romance."

"Why haven't we heard any of this before?" Ada asked. "Especially since I was going to. . ."

Mother's head was shaking so vehemently, Ada feared for her neck. "This is totally inappropriate dinner-table talk. I want—"

Father interrupted. "It's fascinating dinner-table talk, my dear. And I want to hear the answer to Ada's question myself."

Nana and Mr. Alcott exchanged glances, and suddenly their wrinkles fell away and Ada could imagine them as twentysomething youths with America at their feet.

Mr. Alcott continued the story. "Our ship arrived in New York City on August second, so there was a party on board the evening before." He grinned. "Hildegard and I danced until the soles of our shoes begged for relief."

"We danced out of desperation. Our families had divergent plans in America. We didn't know if we'd ever see each other again," Nana said. "And we didn't—for ten years."

"Which was after I married my Emma."

"And after I married my Herbert."

Ada was entranced. To think that her grandmother and Samuel's grandfather had known each other, and loved each other. . .

Mr. Alcott took a spoonful of squash soup and dabbed his mouth with a napkin. "Even Samuel doesn't know of our connection. I planned on sharing all of this with him and your family, but then. . ." He looked around the table, making sure he gave each diner a look. "I must apologize for last year. I'm devastated that Samuel's choice brought such pain to so many."

Ada's father answered. "We appreciate how hard it was on you, too, Nathaniel. I'm just pleased you've had a chance to be reunited—though the conditions are less than ideal."

John piped in. "I do believe Samuel will recover."

"You do?" Ada and Mr. Alcott asked at the same time.

"I do. His body is taking care of first things first, which is resting in order to repair itself."

Ada was glad for John's words.

Then Mother said, "Ada is nearly betrothed to Owen Reed. The Reeds make their fortune in shipping."

Ada was appalled. "Mother! I am not engaged to Owen yet."

"You will be. Mark my words."

"Good for you," Mr. Alcott said. "Do you love him?"

Mother gasped, but Nana nodded, also wanting an answer.

"Forgive me for being so forthright," Mr. Alcott said. "I've wasted too many months holding my tongue. But now that I'm released from my self-imposed prison, I realize there are only so many words left to say, so I shouldn't waste time being coy or subtle."

Nana nodded. "As I always knew, you're a man after my own heart, Nathaniel Alcott."

After an awkward silence, Father turned to John. "Now then. Tell us how things are progressing over at the Academy, son."

The discussion shifted.

Thank You, Father.

**

After dinner Ada stood beside Samuel's bed. Mr. Alcott had gone home but would return tomorrow. Her mother had retired with a headache. And Nana. . . Her grandmother's room was Ada's next stop before retiring for the night.

Ada had given the nurse a break so she could go have some dinner, but mostly because Ada needed this time alone with Samuel. With the story about Nana and Mr. Alcott. . .

Everything had changed.

It wasn't a monumental transformation, but knowing that their grandparents had once loved each other caused a shift in Ada's thinking. When she and Samuel had been together, they'd often shared a common belief that God had brought them together—which had made their split especially painful. *What God has joined together, let no man put asunder.* But now. . .who would have thought a traffic jam and a rearing horse could have been instrumental in bringing Ada and Samuel back into each other's lives? It was an astounding coincidence.

Or not. Perhaps there was no such thing.

Perhaps it was God. Who but the Almighty could have arranged it? And on that very outing, hadn't Ada prayed that she would find Samuel? Perhaps God wasn't through with them yet.

Suddenly Samuel breathed deeper, a long, controlled in and out.

Ada leaned over him, touching his forehead. "Samuel? It's Ada. Please wake up and know me. *Please.*"

But Samuel slept on.

For now.

**

"Come in."

Ada entered Nana's bedroom and found her in her usual spot in bed, leaning against a mountain of pillows. Yet tonight there was something different about the scene.

"You're positively glowing, Nana."

Nana put her palms to her cheeks. "Am I?"

Ada sat on the edge of the bed. "You had quite a surprise for us this evening."

"My, that was fun," she said. "And the look on my daughter's face. . ."

"So Mother didn't know? Any of it?"

Nana shook her head. "When you and Samuel started courting, I crossed paths with Nate as our families began to socialize. But his wife had recently died, and the focus needed to be on you two lovebirds. We occasionally discussed telling the families of our connection, but decided we would wait until after you were betrothed." She shrugged, then smiled. "He's still quite a handsome man, don't you think?"

Ada laughed. "I suppose he is."

Nana snuggled down under the covers. "Turn off the light, child. I'm looking forward to happy dreams."

Chapter Ten

Mr. Alcott spent most of his days by his grandson's bedside, and though Samuel occasionally stirred and even spoke a few incoherent words, he did not fully awaken.

Ada tried to be patient, and she renewed her prayers, thinking that if God saw that she had pulled aside the curtain she'd drawn between herself and the Almighty since last Christmas, He might hear her pleas and fully bring Samuel back to her.

Nana spent her days keeping Mr. Alcott company. Ada often paused at the door to Samuel's room and listened to their happy voices and laughter. They sounded like young people, eager in each other's company. Not at all like a sickly octogenarian or a broken, rumpled man, hidden away in his study. What had changed them?

Love.

Though Ada dared not mention that word in front of her mother — who could

not hide her annoyance toward the two—
Ada knew love *was* the reason for their
transformation. And it gave her hope. If
she loved Samuel enough, and if he still
loved her. . .

Anything was possible.

But first things first. Tonight was her
family's Christmas party. The Wallace
household would be teeming with seventy-
some guests, all dressed in their holiday
best. There would be a seven-course meal,
Christmas caroling, and even some
dancing to a string quartet, hired for the
occasion. Yet in spite of the merriment,
Ada wished she could spend the evening
in Samuel's room with Nana and Mr.
Alcott. Although they were obviously
invited to the party, they had declined for
the sake of propriety. Having Samuel
ensconced in the Wallace home had created
enough brouhaha among their set.
Knowing Nana and Mr. Alcott's past—and
present—relationship would have been too
much for society to bear.

Sadie pinned a sprig of holly in Ada's
hair. "There. How do you like it?"

It was very pretty—and Ada said so. The problem was her heart wasn't in the evening.

Especially since there was the chance that tonight, Owen would propose. She knew it was her mother's fervent wish. And as such, it was Ada's fervent fear. For even though she loved Owen—in a way— with Samuel back in her life. . .she couldn't become engaged to Owen. She just couldn't.

And yet, with Samuel still out of commission, with no words exchanged between them, she couldn't be certain he still loved *her*. What if Owen proposed and she declined, and then Samuel woke up and *he* declined? To enter another Christmas having lost two beaus—one of them twice?

Yet wouldn't it be worse to marry the wrong man?

"Does your head hurt, miss?" Sadie asked, looking at Ada's reflection. "Would you like me to get your some headache powder?"

Ada nodded. It was not a good way to begin a party.

**

"You look very pretty tonight, Ada," Owen said, kissing her cheek. "Merry Christmas."

"Merry Christmas." She forced a smile, hating her mood, knowing Owen didn't deserve her brooding.

"How is Samuel?" he asked.

"He still hasn't fully awakened."

"I'm sorry to hear that."

A few other friends asked after Samuel, but Ada could tell their interest was more prurient in nature than a true concern for his health. They wanted him well so he could talk and add to the gossip by giving details of where he'd been for the past year. They wanted him well so they could shun him.

But as the festivities began, the guests forgot Samuel Alcott was in the house. They mingled and laughed, ate heartily from the mountain of holiday delicacies, sang carols, and danced to the string quartet. Ada went through the motions. She smiled at the appropriate times, offered the appropriate verbal response to every question, and danced with her usual ease, but her heart was elsewhere.

Upstairs. Close, but so very far away.

Ada's mother seemed to be the only one who sensed something was wrong, because the more Ada felt detached from the party, the more frenzied her mother became, flitting from this couple to that one, talking too loudly, laughing too forcibly, and being too much the hostess.

Ada looked toward the stairs longingly. If only she could make a discreet exit.

But then Owen stepped forward among the crowd and clinked a fork against a glass. "Attention, friends! Attention, please."

The musicians ceased, and the room grew quiet as everyone drew close.

"I have an announcement to make."

At first, Ada, wrapped up in her if-only thoughts, felt no premonition of what was to come. But when she saw the beaming face of her mother, she knew a specific plan had been hatched and was about to play out.

No! No, Owen. Don't do it!

But Owen continued. "In this season of love and goodwill, I would like to ask Miss Ada Wallace to be my wife." He took her hand, got down on one knee, and repeated the question. "Ada, would you marry me?"

It was as though Ada were removed from the moment, as if she floated near the coffered ceiling and looked down upon the scene. *Owen's proposing in public? Now?*

Before she could gather herself to figure out if there *was* a way to politely decline, her mother rushed forward and said, "Yes! Of course, Owen! How wonderful!" She held out her glass. "Come, everyone. Toast the happy couple!"

Awkwardly, the guests gained a glass. Owen stood, but his eyes were on Ada, the question still on his face.

But she couldn't say yes. And with seventy guests ready to toast their betrothal, she couldn't say no. Not here. He deserved an explanation, and that wasn't possible here.

"To Owen and Ada!" someone said.

"Hear, hear!"

Hugs and congratulations followed.

What had just happened?

**

The party was over, and thankfully the house was quiet. The guests and Mr. Alcott had returned home. Ada felt wrung out inside, yet she could not retire until she talked with Nana. She found her seated at the dressing table, a maid braiding her waist-length hair in preparation for bed.

"How was the party, child? Tell me all about it."

Ada took over for the maid and waited until she was gone before speaking. "Long ago I promised that you would be the first to know."

It only took Nana a few seconds to understand. She stopped Ada's braiding by facing her. "You're engaged?"

Ada nodded.

"To Owen."

"Of course to Owen. It's not like Samuel has suddenly awakened and proposed."

Nana's shoulders slumped, her forehead strained in deep thought. "You didn't have to say yes."

"And I didn't! Not really." Ada explained what had happened. "And afterward, on more than one occasion, I tried to pull Owen aside to set him straight. But each and every time I had him alone, Mother appeared and pulled us back with the others. It's very clear she instigated the entire proposal. I don't doubt she even assured Owen I would accept, for I can't imagine him proposing in public unless he was sure of my answer."

"What Winifred wants, Winifred gets."

Ada nodded. "Mother was so strong. She just stepped in and —"

"Made it happen."

Ada nodded. "So how can it be fixed?"

Nana put a hand on Ada's, quieting her. "There's only one question that needs to be asked."

"What's that?"

"What do *you* want?"

Immediately Ada's mind became congested with words and thoughts. "I. . .I —"

Nana held up a hand and shook her head. "Shh. Don't say anything now. Life-changing decisions are like tea; they need to steep in hot water in order to develop their full flavor."

"But I'm already in hot water. I'm engaged!"

Nana moved to the bed and snuggled into the pillows. "Turn down the light, child, and bring me some tea in the morning."

**

Ada sat at her dressing table in her nightgown, brushing and rebrushing her hair.

I'm engaged.

Nana's question returned: *What do* you *want?*

She closed her eyes but found Owen's face there—his smile broad as he stood at the door and kissed her cheek good night. "We can choose a ring together, Ada. Your mother thought. . ." He'd finished the evening with a declaration. "I'll make you happy, Ada. I promise."

"No!" Ada threw her brush on the dressing table, knocking over a perfume bottle.

The smell of honeysuckle wafted toward her as she righted it. But it was the only thing that could be righted. . . .

She had no doubt Owen would try to make her happy. He was a good man, a kind man, and up until very recently, she'd thought he was the right man.

And all logic said that was still true. In fact, she'd hoped for a night like this, a festive night where he would propose.

That is, until Samuel came back into her life.

The fact she'd never told Owen *yes* seemed of little import to her friends, to her family, or to Owen. To them the deed was done, the betrothal made. Ada leaned her head on her hands.

She started when her mother entered unannounced, her arms outstretched, her face glowing with gladness. "Ada, my dear daughter. You did it! You really did it."

Before Mother could make contact, Ada turned around on the bench and glared at her. "I didn't do anything, Mother. I didn't even say yes."

Mother took a step back, her hand to her chest. "Of course you did."

"Of course *you* did. *You* stepped in and agreed for me. You didn't give me the chance to answer him—nor to make things right."

"I have no idea what you're talking—"

Ada stood to face her. "You have every idea. In fact, I suspect every detail of this evening was your idea."

Mother tried to veil a smile but was only partially successful. "I'm not going to argue with you, Ada. If, as you say, I answered for you, it's because someone had to take charge and move you forward on your proper path."

"The path *you* think is proper."

"Absolutely. I've seen the look in your eyes since Samuel came back. He spurned you once, Ada. Are you truly waiting for him to awaken so he can spurn you again? Nothing has changed. You might as well live in separate countries for the expanse of class and philosophy that divides you. Owen is one of us. He loves you. And if you'd snap out of your fog, you'd see he's the best thing that's happened to you."

Ada did appreciate Owen for being instrumental in lifting her family out of the pit of society's oblivion. And her mother was right about the fact that nothing had changed in Samuel's situation. As far as she knew, he was still married to his work. But what if his work could also be *her* work? Somehow. Some way?

Mother's face softened, and she took Ada's hands. "Be honest with yourself, daughter. You *do* want to marry Owen Reed, and all this protest is ridiculous. I know your heart has been touched by Samuel, and even by the ridiculous pairing of my mother and Mr. Alcott. But compassion is not passion. Samuel came into your life, and you're helping him. You—"

"He's helped me."

Mother looked skeptical. "He is not of our world. And as soon as he's able, he will return to his world. And you. . .you must let him go."

"But—"

Mother's eyes grew hard. "Listen here. I've worked my entire life to get the Wallace family firmly ensconced into the Four Hundred. Samuel Alcott nearly ruined that for us, and Owen Reed rectified Samuel's mistake. Our mistake. Do you understand?"

Ada had no argument.

No stand.

No way out.

Chapter Eleven

The day after Ada's engagement dawned, and the sun came up. And though she'd always imagined such a day would seem extraordinary and full of anticipation for the future, with this morning came confusion, desperation, and even anger.

She was engaged to a wonderful man, but she resented it.

She was in love with an injured, unresponsive man who might *not* be in love with her, a man who lived and worked in a world set apart from her own.

Ada felt as if she were walking on a rope stretched across a cavern. One false move and she would fall into nothingness, with no hope of surviving unscathed. Yet to stay the course and make it to the other side. . . What waited for her there?

Sadie helped her get dressed, but breakfast was difficult as Mother insisted on talking about the wedding. Invitations, dinner menus, flowers. . .

"And your dress should be covered in Belgian lace. Perhaps we could have Worth in Paris design it."

"Sounds expensive," her father said.

"Of course it does," Mother said. "Of course it *is*. Ada is our only daughter. We only get to do this once."

Nana looked directly at Ada. "Indeed. You only get to do this once."

Once. I only get to marry once. I must make the right choice.

"I suppose you'll be wanting a European tour for your honeymoon?" Father asked.

Mother answered for her. "I'll miss having you gone six months, but it is a must."

And there it was. The tipping point, the one comment that made everything fall into place.

A European honeymoon. . .

The idea of being away from Samuel for six months was unbearable. She couldn't marry Owen and leave. Not when her heart belonged to Samuel.

Ada dropped her fork against the plate and scooted her chair back. "I'm sorry. If you'll excuse me?"

"Excuse you?" Mother said. "We're in the middle of a discussion about your wedding."

She wanted to tell them of her revelation, but she had someone else to tell first. Whether Samuel awakened or not, whether he could hear her or not, she had to declare her love to him.

As Ada moved to the doorway of the dining room, Nana asked, "So the tea is brewed and hot, child?"

Ada paused and nodded. "The tea is steaming and full of flavor."

As she hurried up the stairs, she heard Nana's laughter.

"Tea?" her mother said. "What's all this talk about tea?"

**

Ada burst into Samuel's room and set the nurse free to get her own breakfast.

She rushed to Samuel's side, took his hand, and gave the words release. "I love you, Samuel. I don't know if you love me, but I have never stopped loving you, and I—"

He moaned.

Ada leaned close and stroked his cheek. "Samuel? It's Ada. Come on now. Open your eyes. Wake up. All the way now. Talk to me, Samuel."

As if her wish was his command, Samuel's eyelids fluttered, then opened. He looked at Ada, blinked slowly, then looked again. "Ada? It *is* you."

Ada began to cry. "It is me."

The world was right and good again. *Thank You, God! Thank You!*

She'd made her choice not to marry Owen without knowing how Samuel felt — an all-or-nothing decision. But now, since he was awake, what if he. . .

Ada shook away the thought. The fact was, whether Samuel still loved her or not, her own feelings wouldn't change.

The tea was brewed, and her heart was warm with love.

Neither could be undone.

**

Samuel couldn't take his eyes off her. Ada was more beautiful than he remembered. He could only guess at the extent of the pain he'd caused her during the past year. Yet her smile still had the ability to melt his heart.

He was content to let her explain how he happened to be at the Wallaces'. He had little memory of the accident, and certainly had no memory of all that had come after but for seeing her face and saying her name, once, before falling into the abyss of his injuries.

Yet he *had* seen her before that. "I saw you," he said, after she explained the accident. "I saw you on the street."

"I didn't see you," she said. "Or rather, I saw a man save a little boy but didn't know it was you until you were in the carriage."

"I'd prayed for the chance to see you again," he said.

Her eyes widened. "I prayed to see you, too, on that very outing."

He squeezed her hand, relishing the softness of her skin and the elegant length of her fingers. "It seems clear that God brought us together again."

Her eyes filled with tears, and she cupped his face in her palm. "He did, didn't He?"

Their reunion was interrupted when the door opened and Samuel's grandfather walked in. "Good morning, Ada. How's our patient do—?"

He pulled up short.

"Morning, Grandfather."

The old man rushed toward him, fluttering and flubbering his greetings. Samuel was surprised at his tears and extinguished one as it slid down his grandfather's cheek. "I'm so glad to see you."

"Oh, Samuel, my boy, you'll never know how glad I am to see you."

Ada relinquished her place. "I'll leave you to your celebration. I must spread the good news."

Samuel was reluctant to see her go but took solace in knowing she would return.

If he had his way, they would never be separated again.

**

Ada caught up with her parents in the entry foyer as Wilson helped her father don his coat to go to work. She rushed down the stairs.

"He's awake!" she said. "Samuel's fully awake!"

They all froze for a moment, her father with his arm halfway in the coat's sleeve. Then he said, "Well, good for him. It shows he's on the mend."

Mother's head shook back and forth as if trying to let the news percolate through the soil of her brain. "Yes, good. He can go home now."

Ada felt her jaw drop. "Mother!"

Father adjusted the coat at his shoulders as Wilson stood by with his hat, gloves, and walking stick. "Winifred, really."

Mother reddened but did not change her stance. "I don't mean this very minute, but since he's awake, I'm sure he'd rather go back to his home. After all, Christmas is just a few days away and—"

Her mother's brash words gave Ada the courage to share her own. "I'm not going to marry Owen. I want to marry Samuel."

Father bobbled his hat, and it was recovered by the butler. "You just became engaged to Owen."

"But I've never stopped loving Samuel, and now that he's fully back—"

"He is not back," Mother said. "He is here only because of his injuries. He still lives in some hovel down in the slums. He is still penniless."

Father cocked his head. "I wouldn't count on that anymore, Winifred. From what I've seen of Nathaniel, the fences between grandfather and grandson have been mended."

"Be that as it may," Mother said, "we will not have you shame this family again, daughter. It's bad enough to have one man reject you, but to break it off with yet another man who is actually your fiancé? Our reputation cannot endure it."

Ada turned to her father for support, but he said, "Your mother's right, Ada. Do you honestly want to put your family through another year like the last?"

No, but...

"And this time there may not be an Owen Reed to pull you out of it," Mother said. "Owen is your last chance in society."

"But what if I don't want to be in society anymore?"

Her parents looked as though she'd announced she wanted to die. Father's voice became stern. "You've made a commitment to Owen in front of friends and family. You must follow through. You will follow through."

"But *I* didn't make the commitment — Mother did!"

Father looked from his daughter to his wife, then clinched the entire conversation by putting on his gloves. "You are engaged to Owen Reed. I do business with his father. His family and ours will be bound through your union. Samuel Alcott is a man from your past. Do not confuse sympathy and empathy for love."

"But I do love him."

Father tapped the top of his hat with the brass tip of his walking stick. "I will hear no more of it, Ada. We've done our duty by Samuel. He is awake, and when able, he should return to his life and leave you to yours."

"But Father —"

He left the house, the situation sealed with the closing of the door.

"You see your father agrees with me," Mother said. "You see I'm right."

Ada swept past her and ran up the stairs to Samuel.

To her Samuel.

As she passed her grandmother's room, Nana was coming out. "My, my, what's wrong, child?"

Ada burst into tears and let Nana usher her inside.

**

Samuel reveled in the company of his grandfather. Gone was the gruff man who'd raised him, the man who rarely uttered a kind or encouraging word. The man before him wore his heart on his sleeve, and his heart revealed his love for his grandson. Samuel mourned the deeper wrinkles in his grandfather's face, and knew he was their cause. But the glint in the old man's eyes made up for the extra creases and furrows, revealing a light and life that Samuel had never seen before.

Their reunion was interrupted by the entrance of Mrs. Wallace.

Grandfather stood. "Do you see, Winifred? The dead have come back to life!"

"I see," she said, though her face showed no joy in the fact. "If you don't mind, Mr. Alcott, I would like a few words with your grandson — in private."

Grandfather hesitated and looked to Samuel, who said, "Go on. Perhaps you could see if I might have something to eat. I'm feeling hungry."

His grandfather jumped at the chance to help, and left Samuel alone with Ada's mother.

Samuel was glad for the chance to offer his appreciation. "I'm glad to talk with you, Mrs. Wallace. I want to thank you for taking me in and looking after me while I —"

She stood a goodly length away from the bed, her hands clasped in front of her. "I want you gone, Mr. Alcott."

"What?"

"You've hurt our family once, and you will not hurt us again. I'm glad you're all right, but now it's time to leave. Go away, Samuel Alcott. You must, for Ada's sake. Because she's engaged."

"Engaged?"

"To Owen Reed, a fine, upstanding man of breeding and society, who will love her, cherish her, and care for her in a way you cannot."

"I. . .I didn't know."

"Well, now you do."

With that, she made her exit.

Samuel was left speechless. The joy that had filled him to overflowing at seeing Ada and his grandfather was dashed. But why hadn't Ada said something? Her attentiveness and smile had given him every indication she still loved him as much as he loved her.

For he *did* still love her. Had never stopped loving her.

The past year had been excruciating for Samuel. Although he felt satisfaction in helping the children, he often wondered at the price he'd paid. Had he misread God's leading when he thought God had said *"Wait"* in regard to their engagement?

His own heartache had tested his decision, and when his grandfather had cut him off and they'd become estranged. . . How could so much heartache be God's will? He wasn't the only person who could work with the children—he was never so arrogant as to think that. So had he given up everything for a calling that was *not* his own? And why hadn't he given Ada the chance to join him in his work? She'd offered, but he'd judged her offer as impulsive and unfeasible. He'd virtually deemed her willingness to sacrifice her lifestyle for a life together as insincere.

Who was he to judge her in such a way? To limit her?

But by the time he'd realized the arrogance of his mistake, he'd seen the society pages in a newspaper that mentioned Ada attending a dinner at the Vanderbilts' with Owen Reed — of the Reed shipping fortune.

He'd let her go, and she had moved on without him. And now she was to be Mrs. Owen Reed.

It was too late. He'd experienced true love but had tossed it aside, unmindful of its value. *"Who can find a virtuous woman? for her price is far above rubies."* Samuel had found such a woman but had not been willing to pay the price to keep her.

He stared into the fire, letting the flicker of the flames take his mind back to the days before the accident. Ada had been on his mind more than usual. As he'd gone about his work, trying to make some wooden toys for the children for Christmas, trying to keep the foundling home supplied with firewood and food, his thoughts had returned to Ada. They always returned to Ada. Her face. Her smile. Her loving eyes. Her soft skin, and the completeness he felt when she was in his arms.

And when he'd seen her alight from the carriage in Five Points, it was as if an angel had touched down in a dark world — his dark world. The children, the horse, the screams, the pain. . .he would suffer them all again if it would bring her back into his life.

But to have found her, only to lose her?

His thoughts burned away in the flames, leaving the images of Ada in the ashes.

**

After telling Nana about all that had transpired, Ada let her grandmother's arms enfold her. "You always know how to comfort me, Nana."

"It's my job, child."

Ada sat upright. "So what should I do? I chose Samuel, and now he's awake. But Father says—"

"You are to honor your parents."

It was not what Ada wanted to hear. "Even if they're wrong?"

"They are not *wrong*. Owen is a wonderful man, and in spite of your feelings, your father has laid down his decision."

"What about brewing tea? What about coming to my own life-changing decision?"

"Ultimately, whether you like it or not, you are under your father's authority."

Ada stood, her frustration requiring movement. "If I have no power, then why did you urge me to make my own choice?"

Nana put a hand to her forehead, rubbing the space between her eyes. "Perhaps I was wrong to offer you an option where there was none. Perhaps I was caught up in the fantasy of true love and happy endings."

"Fantasy? So my feelings aren't real? And it doesn't matter what I choose?"

"In the end, probably not."

"But that's not fair!" Ada knew she sounded like a petulant child but didn't care.

"Life isn't fair, child. Was it fair that Nathaniel and I lost track of each other and were directed to marry others? I think not."

Ada was surprised by her grandmother's admission. "So you regret marrying Grandfather?"

" ' 'Tis better to have loved and lost, than never to have loved at all.' " That said, Nana shook her head. "Regrets have sharp teeth, child. And I *did* grow to love your grandfather." She put her hand beneath Ada's chin. "Without him I would not have you."

"But what if. . . ?"

Nana shook her head. "A life can drown in what-ifs. After seeking God's counsel and guidance, we must make the best decisions we can amid the barriers that exist around us. Beyond that, we must look forward instead of back."

"But you've found Mr. Alcott again. You're getting a second chance."

Decades fell from Nana's face. "God is good—all the time. And He's often full of surprises."

"If God brought Mr. Alcott back into your life to love, doesn't it follow that He brought Samuel back into my life to love?"

"Time will tell."

But time was the problem. Her mother would see to it that Samuel left as soon as possible.

Time was running out.

Or was the hourglass already empty?

**

By the time Ada returned to Samuel's room, he was sitting up and his grandfather was feeding him some soup.

"Look, Ada. He's eating," Mr. Alcott said.

"I told him I could do it myself, but he insists."

Ada's smile seemed wistful. Almost distant. Had something happened to upset her?

"You've grown weak," she said. "We fed you when we could, but you were asleep more than awake, and often delirious."

"Until this morning when I awakened and saw you." He smiled, then looked away. He had to be careful not to be too familiar. She was not his anymore. "I'm going home tomorrow."

Ada hesitated, her face tormented. Then she nodded. "I'm sure they're worried about you. I would have sent word, but I never knew exactly where you were."

He'd kept the location and name of the foundling home a secret from her — and his grandfather. It had seemed right at the time. He hadn't wanted either to seek him out and make his decision harder, but now he thought of Eliza and the children. What must they be thinking since he hadn't returned?

Mr. Alcott handed Samuel a napkin to wipe his chin. "I think leaving tomorrow is being hasty, Samuel. Dr. Wallace hasn't even seen you yet. He may say you can't go."

Samuel found Ada's eyes and held her gaze. "I must go."

Her forehead furrowed. Samuel wasn't sure if Ada was aware that he knew of her engagement. His visit from Mrs. Wallace had seemed clandestine, as if Ada's mother had wanted him to know Ada was promised to another—because she guessed Ada wouldn't tell him herself. He wished Ada *would* tell him. For until he heard the words from her mouth, he would always cling to a glimmer of hope. And until he heard the words, he could *not* declare his love.

His need for the air to be cleared took over. "Is there something you'd like to tell me, Ada?"

He watched her eyes flicker, as if matching the fire of her thoughts.

Tell me. If you love another, set me free. If not. . .tell me you love me and let me soar.

She finally said, "I'm going to miss you, Samuel. It was so wonderful to see you again."

Samuel dissected her words. Did her omission of the facts mean she didn't consider herself truly engaged? Or perhaps she was trying to be kind, thinking that her betrothal would hurt him.

"This going-home business," Grandfather said. "If anything, you should come home with me. You need more care. And I—"

Samuel put a hand on his grandfather's, stopping his words. "I need to return to the place where I belong."

"But I just got you back. You can't leave me again."

"I must." Samuel's throat tightened. He would have liked nothing better than to stay in the company of these people he loved. But he'd strayed beyond the boundaries of his domain, and it was time to return to it.

Lord, please help me do this.

Chapter Twelve

I'm going home today.

Samuel looked around the guest room for the last time. He would miss the people who had visited him here. Ada and Grandfather, Mrs. Bauer, and John.

Not Mrs. Wallace.

He couldn't get the image of Ada's mother out of his mind. Or her command: *"Go away, Samuel Alcott."*

He understood why she hated him. In many ways he hated himself.

But Ada. . . He doubted he would ever love again. Not in that way. He loved the children as his own, and loved Eliza as the big sister he'd never had, but he knew that the part of his heart reserved for a wife, a partner, and a soul mate was closed. Whether by God's design or his own folly, the door was locked, the key misplaced.

With a hand to his sore ribs, he stood and held the bedpost for support. He'd done a good job of convincing John he was well enough to return to Five Points. But the truth was far less certain. He hated to be a burden to Eliza, but he had to leave here and stop this torture.

He thought back to the carriage, to the first time he'd opened his eyes and had seen Ada looking back at him. In his delirium during the days that followed, he'd heard her voice. She'd been the one to guide him through his haze into clarity. He'd even felt her touch and had taken comfort in it. If only he could hold her one more time, kiss her—

Stop it! She belongs to another man. You rejected her. You caused all this. You. . .

Are a fool.

**

Getting Samuel home became a production. John was going along as a doctor—to help Samuel negotiate the carriage and to inform those on the other end as to Samuel's medical needs.

Mr. Alcott had insisted on going, for he wanted to see this foundling home that had stolen his grandson's loyalty.

And Nana, who hadn't been out of the house in over two years, was going along because Mr. Alcott was going. Plus, she'd always had a soft heart for children.

And finally Ada, who had never imagined seeing Samuel to his destination, became a part of the farewell party — in spite of her mother's protests. This — at least she could have this.

The seating arrangement in the carriage was exactly to Ada's preferences. John sat outside with the coachman, leaving room for Mr. Alcott and Samuel with their backs to the horses and the ladies facing them. Although Ada would have liked to feel Samuel's arm against hers, to be able to see him, knowing within a short time she might never see him again. . .

It was bittersweet, but better than nothing.

She looked at the two men sitting across from her. They were members of the same family tree, a tree with wealthy roots. Yet they had ventured onto two very different branches, each with its own distinct purpose and reach.

The world needed both of them. Mr. Alcott's entrepreneurship was the sap that made America grow and flourish. He created jobs. And as a banker he loaned other entrepreneurs money to go after their dreams. Without this type of ingenuity and risk-taking, the working class would all fall into poverty.

Poverty. Five Points. Children without a home.

Ada looked at Samuel and received a wistful smile. Samuel had chosen an upper branch, one not often touched by human hands. But were the fruits of his labors any less important simply because they were less seen? To take care of children, to help them trust again, to help them feel of worth, was a fruit that could reap riches beyond measure. Who knew what those children would do or be when they grew up? Would one of them become president? Or create some invention that would change the world? Or fall in love and marry and have a houseful of children of their own?

This last bounty was priceless, yet harder to measure than the success that revealed itself on ledger sheets. Ada was going to marry Owen. They would have children. The parade of generations would go on. To be fair, she knew she should tell Samuel about her betrothal, but she couldn't bring herself to do it. To tell him the truth would forever separate them.

Distance would accomplish that of its own accord.

"What's got you thinking so deeply, Miss Wallace?" Mr. Alcott asked.

"Oh, nothing."

Oh, everything.

**

Samuel led the way up the steps of the foundling home. He was nervous. How would Ada and Grandfather react to it? Would they be repulsed by what they'd see? Or would their hearts be softened? He knew it didn't really matter, but he still wanted them to understand why he had given them up.

"This is it," he said, leading the group inside. He nearly made apologies in advance, but stopped himself. There were no apologies to be made. It was what it was.

Eliza came into the small entry foyer from the kitchen, wiping her hands on an apron. "Samuel!"

She ran toward him and encased him

in a rocking embrace that caused him pain—which he disguised. "Where have you been? Are you all right?" she asked. She gently touched a cut on his face.

"I had an accident with a horse. The Wallaces took me in and cared for me." He didn't go into more details. There was plenty of time for that.

The children heard the ruckus and came rushing from all corners of the house, hugging his legs and wrapping their arms around his waist. "Papa Samuel! You're back!"

"Ich verfehlte Sie."

"Sono felice che siete bene."

Samuel put his hands on their heads and told them he'd missed them, too. Home. He was home. There was nothing like it.

"Back, children. Back," Eliza said. "Give him room to breathe." Eliza finally gave her attention to the others. "And who have we here?"

Mr. Alcott removed his hat and gave her a bow. "Good day, ma'am. I am Nathaniel Alcott, Samuel's grandfather."

Eliza bobbed a curtsy. "Very nice to meet you, I'm sure."

Samuel took over the introductions, taking Ada's arm and moving her close. "Eliza Hathaway, this is Ada Wallace."

Eliza's eyes grew large, and she looked to Samuel for confirmation that this was *the* Ada Wallace. Samuel nodded.

"Very nice to meet you, Miss Wallace. I've heard so many wonderful things about you."

Samuel checked Ada's reaction. She seemed perplexed, as if she couldn't imagine Samuel saying anything nice about her. That made him sad.

Mrs. Bauer stepped forward. "And I am Ada's grandmother, and this"—she drew John forward—"this is my grandson, John. Dr. John Wallace. He's been caring for Samuel."

John offered a bow. "Nice to meet you, ma'am."

"Glad to meet all of you."

"You have quite a gaggle there," John said, pointing to the children.

Samuel looked to Ada as he answered. "These are my children."

"Plus one," Eliza said, nodding to a little girl who stood away from the others on the bottom stair. "I found her yesterday, hiding under the stairs in the alley. Her name is Francesca. She's Italian."

Samuel nudged his way through the children and went to sit on the bottom step. He didn't move to hug her, knowing that many of these children were wary of contact. *"Ciao, Francesca. Il mio nome è Samuel. Il felice voi sono qui."*

"My goodness," Ada said. "You know Italian?"

Once again Eliza answered for him. "Living where we do, we've both had to learn a little Italian, German, French, Russian—"

"And Yiddish," Samuel said. "I learn enough to make the children feel welcome. But they are doing the hard work. All of them are learning English."

"I admire your ear for languages," Mr. Alcott said. "I can barely order from a French menu. I have no talent for it at all."

"Neither did I," Samuel said. "Until I had no choice." He patted the stair, inviting Francesca to sit next to him. She did so, and he touched her raven-black hair. It was as soft as silk.

Eliza clapped her hands. "Come, children. Time for your English lesson with

Mama Lottie." The children ran into the parlor nearby and Ada could see rows of mismatched chairs, all facing in one direction. A young woman stood at the front with a chalkboard in hand. Little Francesca left Samuel's side to join the others.

"Would you like some coffee?" Eliza asked.

"That would be wonderful," John said.

"And I'd like a tour," Mr. Alcott said. "Show us around, Samuel. I want to see everything."

Samuel was surprised by his grandfather's interest, but glad for it. "Come. I'll show you where the children sleep."

As they headed upstairs, Mrs. Bauer took the railing with one hand and Mr. Alcott's arm with the other. "Are you coming, Ada?"

"Of course."

**

Samuel swept an arm toward the hallway. "We have four bedrooms on this floor, and there are two rooms in the attic, one for children and one for me. Eliza stays in a room off the kitchen, and Lottie is married and lives elsewhere. That's the extent of our operation. Nothing fancy."

Ada walked by doorways that revealed small but neat rooms crowded with cots, beds, and bedrolls, three to a room.

"Very nice," she said, though *nice* was an exaggeration. She saw rags shoved between the window sash and sill. A child had drawn a face in the frost on the inside of the glass. It was starting to snow. "This room has nice light."

"A few rooms don't have any windows at all, so this one is prized." Samuel moved to the end of the hall. "Let me show you the attic. Some of the girls have spruced up their room with bits of tin."

"Tin?"

"Come. I'll show you."

Samuel led the way up a narrow staircase. Among the eaves there were two rooms, one on either side. He pointed to the left. "See there? The girls have taken it upon themselves to make their room prettier. They find bits of metal and old cans on the street, flatten them, and punch designs in the tin."

One wall was their gallery, showcasing their odd art. It was an admirable attempt to create beauty where none had been before.

"And this is my room," he said, pointing to the room on the other side of the small landing. "It's small and unadorned. Hardly a place for. . ." He looked to the floor and let the sentence die.

He'd deemed the room unworthy of *her*.

Ada took a step inside the room. The space was smaller than the girls' portion of the attic, the furniture scuffed and in need of paint. A dresser, bed, bedside table, washbasin and pitcher, and chair. The room was the size of her bathroom back home.

She didn't dare ask about those facilities — if there were any.

"I suppose this is very disappointing to all of you," he said. "And incomprehensible."

Ada wasn't sure what to say. For *this* he'd given her up, given up his own family, his inheritance, and his way of life.

"You are one in a thousand men,

Samuel Alcott," Nana said.

"Among thousands of children who need my help. If only we could help them all."

With Mr. Alcott's help, Nana sat on the one chair. " 'Suffer the little children to come unto me, and forbid them not: for of such is the kingdom of God.' "

Samuel smiled. "Exactly."

His grandfather took a deep breath. "I smell coffee. Shall we?"

As they had to descend the attic stairs in single file, Ada purposely held back in order to have a moment with Samuel. "I'm glad you showed me all this," she said when they were alone.

"So you understand?"

She couldn't honestly answer him in the affirmative. She understood the need; she saw the good they were doing. But the sacrifice. . .

He touched her arm. "Ada? Do you understand why I gave up everything to be here?"

She touched his hand with her gloved fingers. "I'm trying to."

**

Samuel followed Ada downstairs. He was glad she'd come, but was dismayed that she still didn't understand his choice, that his rejection of her was because of something bigger than them both. And that even though he loved her, he'd made the right choice.

Because the foundling home was no place for Ada.

As they descended the main staircase to the first floor, he fought this statement. Who was he to say such a thing? God had a purpose in mind for Ada, just as He'd led Samuel to *his* destiny. Now that she'd seen the home, seen the need, seen the children, the seed had been planted.

But she's going to be married to a wealthy man. She's going to live the life she's always known.

The entire issue was too much for Samuel to dissect.

It was up to Ada to water the seed or let it perish.

Lord, guide her.

**

"Well now," Eliza said as Ada and Samuel came into the parlor. "There you are. Did you enjoy your tour?"

"Very much."

Eliza responded, but Ada didn't hear because she was enraptured by the sight of Nana starting a game of cat's cradle with a little girl.

"I see you've met Nusa again," Samuel said.

"Shh!" Nana said as she carefully pinched the right strings to continue the game. "I haven't done this in years. . . ." She successfully completed the transfer, and it was Nusa's turn.

Nusa. The little girl saved by Samuel a year ago. The little girl who'd opened his eyes to the needs of all children. The little girl who'd been instrumental in the destruction of Ada's future with the man she loved.

Ada suffered a shiver. It was too coincidental. Only somehow it wasn't.

"Ohhh! *Ich ließ es fallen!*" Nana dropped the cat's cradle and Nusa laughed.

Ada's thoughts swam. Everyone seemed so at ease here, as if they'd come a hundred times before.

She felt no ease, only confusion. And the need to leave. Immediately.

"We should go," she said.

Eliza held forth a cup. "But you haven't had your coffee."

Ada shook her head, feeling claustrophobic. "I need air." She apologized and rushed outside.

Samuel followed her. A gentle snow fell, dotting their shoulders.

"Ada, why are you upset?"

How could she explain the complexity of her thoughts? "I'm thrilled to have seen you again, Samuel. And I admire the work you're doing here. As Nana said, you are one man in a thousand."

He reached forward and touched her hand. "But I am still just a man. And I. . ." He took a fresh breath. "I wish you every future happiness, Ada."

With that, he returned inside. The visit cut short, the others passed him on their way out, calling their good-byes.

The coachman helped Ada into the carriage. She wanted to be quickly gone.

Away from this place. From him. To leave would cause pain, but to linger. . .

As the carriage moved away from the curb, she felt all eyes on her. "You were rude, child," Nana said. "What got into you?"

She shook her head and looked out the window.

"I, for one, was very impressed," Mr. Alcott said. "Yes, the conditions are minimal and bare, but the children seem happy."

"And healthy," John said. "I offered Miss Hathaway my services if there is ever a need."

Their acceptance and good opinions only added to Ada's inner turmoil.

**

After dropping Mr. Alcott at his home, and John at the Academy, Ada helped Nana upstairs.

"I've tackled more stairs in this one day than I've tackled in a year," Nana said, gripping the massive walnut railing.

"To think that until recently, you rarely came down."

"Silly me. Learn from my mistakes, child. If you give up on life, life will give up on you."

It was the perfect segue. "Giving up on life. . .that's what I need to talk to you about."

At the landing, Nana paused, her eyebrows high. "The visit today affected you?"

"How could it not? Let's talk in your room."

Once there, Ada shut the door, poked the fire to life, and placed a blanket over her grandmother's legs as she sat by the fire. Ada took a seat in a facing chair and plunged ahead.

"It was hard seeing the foundling home," Ada said.

"A fact you made perfectly clear. Rushing out of there as if the entire place was below your dignity. . . Really, Ada."

"But it wasn't that."

"Oh, wasn't it?"

Fine. She'd deal with her reservations first. "They had rags stuffed in the windows and frost on the inside."

Nana pointed to her own bedroom windows. "Go over there. If you move aside the draperies, what do you see?"

Ada pulled aside the massive brocade. "There's frost on the windows."

"Glass is glass, child. *We* have draperies to block the draft. They have rags. Your next objection?"

"They're not objections, Nana. Just observations."

"Such as. . . ?"

"The beds. . .many of them are mere cots with only a thin blanket as a covering."

"And. . . ?"

"And Samuel's room up in the attic. . .it was tiny. There aren't even proper walls. Just open beams and studs and —"

Nana rolled her eyes. "Did you only see what they didn't have, and not see what they *did* have?"

Ada hated that Nana thought badly of her. "Of course I saw what they have. They have each other, and I know love trumps all the not-haves I can name."

Nana seemed to relax. "Now that's a proper observation."

"I tried to think of myself there — for a year ago I *had* offered to go with him."

"And?"

This is where it got difficult. "I actually think I would have grown used to the simpler conditions. If I would have been with Samuel, I'm not sure much of that would have mattered."

"Good for you." She studied Ada's face. "But something else is bothering you."

"I don't know anything about children."

"What's to know? Children are simple creatures. They need food in their stomachs, a roof over their heads, and clothes on their bodies. But most of all, they need attention and love."

She made it sound so simple. Ada fingered the braid on her skirt and moved on to the next issue. "After seeing it all. . .I do think I understand why Samuel chose that life. In fact, I'm kind of jealous."

"Now there's an unexpected twist."

"I know. It surprised me, too," Ada said. "What struck me is that Samuel lives a life full of deep emotions. He felt called by God to this purpose. He felt it so deeply he gave up everything." She cocked her head, her cheeks warming. "I'd like to feel things so deeply. I don't want to give up on life. I don't want to settle. And I'd like God to call me to some purpose."

Nana leaned forward and patted Ada's hand. "Maybe He just has."

Really?

Ada was glad there was a back to her chair. "But Father and Mother insist I marry Owen."

"The way I see it, the call of the heavenly Father usurps any earthly one."

Ada was shocked by Nana's turnaround. "So you want me to disobey them?"

"I want you to take a breath, calm down, and pray about it. Ask God to show you His plan."

Her mind swam with possibilities. And yet there was one hitch. . . . "Samuel never told me he still loves me."

"Did you tell him you still love him?"

Ada scrolled through their conversations since he'd awakened. "After the engagement I realized I did love him, and I made my choice. I wanted to be with Samuel, and I marched into his room to tell him—asleep or no. And I did tell him I love him. But then he woke up, and I worried about what he felt toward me, and then my parents ordered me to marry Owen, and Mother insisted he leave, and. . .it all happened so fast."

"Then slow it down, child. Ask God the questions, and give Him time to arrange the answers."

"Arrange the answers?"

" 'God works in mysterious ways, His wonders to perform.' "

Ada could hear the music of the familiar hymn in her head. An excitement stirred inside her. To anticipate God's leading. . .

She suddenly stood. "I have to go."

Nana smiled "And. . . ?"

"I'll let you know what He says."

Chapter Thirteen

It was just a few days before Christmas, and Ada's time was spent in a whirl. Praying and looking for God's answers consumed her thoughts, even as life went on.

There were Christmas parties to attend, and a caroling excursion. She'd even taken out her bridal quilt, hoping that by looking at its evidence of her life's journey, God would give her some direction. Should she finish the last row of blocks with scraps from the dress she wore the night Owen proposed, or the dress she was wearing on the day of Samuel's accident?

Knowing there was no answer — yet — she decided to use her energy to make a crazy quilt pillow with the appropriate scraps — the dress from the accident, the dress she wore to see the foundling home, and even scraps from the torn shirt Samuel had worn when he'd been injured. She worked on it in secret, feeling joy in each stitch.

Surely that meant something. Was it a sign from God?

It was certainly a start. But time was ticking by, and life was moving on around her.

Unless God gave her immediate direction, it was necessary she buy Owen a gift for Christmas. She took a trip to Bloomingdale's, where she looked at pocketknives, pipes, a brass match safe, and pocket watches. Nothing seemed quite right. The idea of a pipe was rejected because she'd never seen Owen smoke. The match safe—although pretty—was a bit utilitarian, and the pocket watch too intimate. So she had the pocketknife monogrammed. It was the least she could do.

It was the most she could do.

Ada sat in the parlor and finished stitching a small gift bag for the knife. Her brother, John, was in the foyer, dressing up warmly to venture over to the Medical Academy. But before he could leave, there was a knock on the door. Wilson answered it and received a note.

Ada set her stitching aside. Her stomach executed a small flip, as if God. . . "Who's it for?" she asked.

But by then the butler had handed the note to John. "It's for me, sister," he said, unfolding it. He read the note, then looked at her. "It's from Samuel."

Ada's stomach flipped a second time, and she hurried to his side. "What does he say? What does he want?"

John read the note aloud. " 'Dear John, Some of the children are sick. We would greatly appreciate your medical help as soon as possible. Sincerely, Samuel.' "

"Sick children? You're going, aren't you?" she asked.

He donned his hat and began to put on his gloves. "How can I *not* go?"

How can you *not go?*

Ada obeyed the inner nudge. "I'm going with you."

"I can't let you do that, sister. They're sick."

"I've helped with Nana for years, and wasn't I a help to you when you treated Samuel?"

John paused a moment, scrutinizing her. "There's a risk, Ada."

"I'm healthy. I can handle—"

"The risk I was talking about has nothing to do with your health."

So her struggle in regard to Samuel was not a secret. She stepped closer to her brother, speaking low, for his ears alone. "I want to go there again, John. I need to go."

He searched her eyes, then nodded. "I hope you know what you're doing."

God knew. And that was enough.

**

Eliza spooned out oatmeal. She filled three bowls on a tray and handed it to Samuel to take to the sick children upstairs.

"Do you think Dr. Wallace is coming?" she asked him.

"I hope so."

"The children aren't *that* sick, Samuel. . . ."

"I just want to make sure." He turned toward the front hall and the stairs.

But Eliza called after him, "Do you think Ada will come, too?"

Samuel pretended not to hear.

**

"Would you please stop pacing, Samuel?" Eliza asked. "I'm trying to give the children a lesson, and you're distracting them."

Samuel stopped in place and looked at the children being taught their alphabet. All eyes were on him instead of on their teacher.

"Sorry." He moved his pacing to the hall beside the stairway. This waiting was a complete waste of his time, for he had no idea if the note had even reached John, or if he'd had time to divert his day to include Five Points, or whether Ada would even know about the note at all. What if John got the note and left immediately, not even telling his sister of his destination? What if John didn't come? What if John did come but came alone?

"Why didn't I just send Ada a note?"

Hearing his words said aloud caused his pacing to stop. "What have I done? What was I thinking?"

He sank onto the stairs, put his head in his hands, and questioned the whole thing. Ada was on his mind—constantly. The need to see her again was a gaping hole that remained unfilled. So when three of the children had taken sick, he'd concocted the scheme to get her here. Hopefully.

But even if she comes, it doesn't mean she'll stay, or that she'll return your love. She's still engaged to be married. Until that changes, none of your feelings matter.

Samuel raked his fingers through his hair. This is how his thoughts had been since Ada had left, a cacophony of hopes and admonitions rattling against each other, never still.

He prayed under his breath. "Lord, forgive me for taking matters into my own hands. But I love her so. I just want to be with her."

A still, small voice broke through the mental chaos. *"Now. Now, Samuel."*

He sat upright. He dared not make a sound, expel a breath, or move a muscle. *Now?* he prayed.

"Now."

The knock on the door made him jump. His heart beat wildly. He stood and moved his hand toward the door handle. If he opened the door and it was Ada. . .

And there she was, her cheeks flushed from the cold and the journey, her golden curls contained by a gray wool bonnet adorned with a sprig of holly.

"You came," he managed.

"I came," she said.

John cleared his throat. "I came, too. You sent for a doctor?"

Samuel felt himself redden. "Yes, thank you. I'm so glad. Come in and examine the children."

Samuel's thoughts continued to spin — but with gratitude. *Thank You, God. Thank You for. . .now.*

**

"They should be fine," John said, latching his medical bag. "Give them plenty of fluids and rest, and keep the other children away as much as possible."

"Thank you, Doctor," Samuel said. "I'm much relieved." He turned to Ada. "And thank you, Ada, for coming to assist."

Ada accepted his thanks, even though she hadn't done much. To make herself feel useful, she smoothed the covers around the oldest boy, Tito, and stroked his hair away from his forehead.

"Grazie, signorina," he said.

Ada melted. "You're welcome, Tito."

"Sleep, children," Samuel told them. "I'll be up to check on you in a little while."

As they went downstairs, John said, "Send me a note again if you need me. But honestly, I think they'll be much improved even by tomorrow."

Suddenly Ada panicked. Their mission was complete. They were leaving. But they'd just arrived — *she'd* just arrived.

She couldn't leave yet.

Couldn't.

Wouldn't.

In the foyer she made her declaration. "I want to stay and help — if it's all right with Samuel and Eliza, of course."

Samuel beamed, and Eliza came out of the kitchen. "Did I hear an offer to help?"

Ada could have kissed her. "I offered to stay, if you could use me."

Eliza put a finger to her chin and looked to the ceiling. "Let me see. . .thirteen children, three sick in bed, with rooms to rearrange so others won't get sick, and bread to make, and Christmas two days away. . ." She looked at Ada and smiled. "I would much appreciate your help. In fact, how are you in the kitchen?"

"We'll see." Ada kissed her brother on the cheek. "I'm needed here, John."

But before she could escape, he pulled her into the parlor and spoke for her ears alone. "Come home, Ada."

"I can't come home. There's work to be done. Samuel needs me. The children need me."

"Owen needs you. Mother needs you. At home." He glanced at Eliza, who was wiping the nose of a little girl. "Home, Ada. Not here, playing nanny and nursemaid."

"I am not needed at home, brother, and you know it. If I go home right now, how would I spend my day? Reading a book? Listening to Mother press me for ideas about my wedding?"

"You've waited a lifetime for such a wedding."

She had. From the time she'd been old enough to consider the opposite sex more interesting than annoying, she'd daydreamed about a big wedding, marrying an important man of breeding and station.

Yet recently she'd been praying for God's direction. . . .

Ada looked to the foyer. Samuel held a little girl who was playing with his collar. The sight of him was like an answer to her prayer. "Come get me Christmas Day, John. Until then, I want to be here where I'm needed."

"Ada, do you know what you're doing?" he asked.

The answer was no, but she left him to ponder the question on his own. She hurried to the foyer, nudging Eliza toward the kitchen. "Teach me how to make bread, Eliza. I'd love to learn."

Her heart beat in her throat and did not relax until she heard the front door close.

Samuel came into the kitchen. Was he going to argue with her decision?

But he just stood there looking at her.

Say something. Please say something.

"I'm glad you're here," he finally said. "Very glad."

Eliza stepped between them, handing Ada an apron. "Get off with you, Samuel, or I'll find an apron for you, too. If I'm not mistaken, we need more firewood."

He smiled and took up the wood sling. "I'll be back soon."

They were wonderful words, full of promise.

**

Samuel strode down the street, grinning like a madman, his open coat flapping against the wind, his face enveloped by the puffs of his breath in the cold.

Cold he did not feel.

For he was warm inside, glowing and on fire with happiness. Ada was staying! She'd volunteered to stay!

God was good! God was amazing!

He added a joyful jig to his step, receiving a laugh from Mrs. O'Connor, who was selling tin cups in a pushcart nearby. "What's made you so happy today, Samuel Alcott?"

"Christmas," he said. "Merry Christmas!"

**

"You're glowing, Miss Wallace," Eliza said.

Ada wiped the back of her hand across her forehead, trying to rid it of loose hairs. "I'm not glowing; I'm just plain hot. And please call me Ada."

Ada ladled another bowl of stew and handed it down the row of children seated around the table. Older children held younger ones on their laps and blew on each spoonful before helping it reach an eager mouth.

Eliza pulled a pan of baking powder biscuits from the oven. The smell of hot bread was enticing, and Ada's stomach growled.

But her own hunger could wait. The children came first. And oddly. . .she didn't mind.

Which was a revelation of sorts. She couldn't remember the last time she'd felt a hunger pang, or when she'd truly needed something. She also couldn't remember the last time she'd perspired because of exertion rather than the weather.

A *whoosh* of cold air blew in, and she heard the front door close and snow being stomped off boots. She stopped her spooning to look to the hall, eager to see Samuel.

He entered the kitchen with a sling full of wood. His eyes sought hers, and he smiled as though the sight of her truly pleased him. His cheeks were bitten by the cold, and once he set the new wood by the stove, he stood over it, warming his hands. Ada waited for him to say something.

But he didn't.

And she didn't. She wasn't sure what to say. She was in his world; she'd invited herself in. Partly. But Samuel had been the one to send for her brother. Had he wanted her to come along, or was her appearance a surprise?

Did he want her here? He'd said as much, but were they merely polite words? Samuel was usually talkative. They'd never had trouble making conversation before.

Eliza glanced at him, then at Ada. "Gracious sakes, Samuel. Cat got your tongue? Say something nice to our new volunteer—who's just made biscuits for the very first time."

His eyes skimmed over the bread but landed on Ada. "She's full of surprises."

Now he was being ridiculous. Ada spooned out the last bowl of soup and, nudging past him, replaced the pot on the stove. "They're just biscuits, Samuel. And the surprise might be that you like them."

He plucked one from the pan and took an enormous bite, all the while having his eyes locked on hers. "Mmm, good," he said, with crumbs falling to his chin.

Ada brushed a crumb away, then took a seat at the table. On a whim, she reached for a toddler who was sitting on the lap of an older girl, then took up a spoonful of stew, blew on it, and fed it to the child. *See? I can fit in here. I'm up to the challenge.*

Samuel merely laughed and sat at the opposite end of the table.

Eliza shook her head. "My oh my. Life just got interesting."

Indeed.

**

"I hope you don't mind sharing the bed with me," Eliza said. "The good news is I tend to sleep like a corpse with my hands clasped over my chest, so you won't have to nudge me over to my side."

Ada stood before the narrow bed, swimming in one of Eliza's nightdresses. "I told you I could sleep on the settee in the parlor."

"Nonsense. A proper bed brings a proper sleep." Eliza gathered two bricks by the fire with tongs and wrapped them in pieces of flannel. She carried them to the bed and slid them down to the foot end. "There," Eliza said. "That'll take the chill off the sheets. Get in now, and I'll blow out the light."

Once they were settled, once Ada's eyes had adjusted to the moonlight and the low embers of the fire, Eliza said, "Care to pray with me?"

"Of course," Ada said. *Absolutely.*

"Our Father, who art in heaven, hallowed be Thy name. Thy kingdom come. . ."

Thy will be done.

**

Samuel tucked in the last of the children. It was a nightly ritual that never grew old. To see each one safely in bed, their angelic faces nestled against the pillows, gave him a satisfaction that was full and warm and complete.

Well, not entirely complete. For tonight when he returned to the house and saw Ada there, helping the children, at ease and hard at work, he'd felt his usual satisfaction swell to a new level. It had taken all his self-control not to drop the wood with a thud and a thump, rush to her, and take her in his arms — where he would never let her go.

That's why he'd been so tongue-tied; he'd feared his surge of emotions would envelop them both and scare her away. God had been very generous in bringing her back to him. Samuel didn't want to ruin things by moving too fast.

But you only have two days. . . .

"Patience is a virtue," he whispered to himself.

"What you say, Papa Samuel?" Nusa asked.

He shook his head and smiled at the girl who'd started him on this journey. Then he kissed her forehead. "Sleep well, Nusa. God bless you."

God bless us all.

Ada's eyes shot open. Then she flinched as she saw the eyes of a child at bed level, staring at her. She remembered the little girl's name. "Sara Christine? What's wrong?"

"I had a bad dream."

Ada opened the covers. "Everything will be all right. Come in here with us."

The little girl climbed in bed, but quickly crawled over Ada to the center spot between Ada and Eliza. Ada turned over and saw Eliza's eyes gleaming in the moonlight. "Welcome to my world," she whispered.

As Sara Christine snuggled her head onto Ada's pillow, Ada pulled the child close and reveled in her warmth. She felt her throat grow tight at the perfection of the moment, of holding another person close, of providing comfort, of. . .of. . .

Of offering love and feeling loved in return.

Chapter Fourteen

"You're a good bed-maker, Mama Ada."

Ada mitered the final corner and stood. She stared at her helper, twelve-year-old Brigid. "Mama Ada?"

Brigid shrugged. "You don' mind, do ya? That's what the kids is calling ya."

Ada shook her head no. Yet back with her family *she* was the child.

Back home *she* didn't have to work.

Ada handed Brigid a stack of sheets. "Take these to the next room. I'll be with you in a minute." Once alone, she sank onto the bed.

It was all very confusing. She'd been at the children's home less than a day, helping to take care of the children, helping the children learn to take care of themselves. Both Samuel and Eliza had told her she didn't have to help so much, but she'd wanted to. She'd needed to.

And yet *she'd* had to be taught how to make a bed, to do the wash, to make bread to sell in a pushcart on the street along with some wooden toys that Samuel whittled. Two older boys did the actual selling, so at least there wasn't *that* task. She'd learned how to change diapers, and this afternoon she was going to learn how to teach the alphabet and arithmetic. Eliza had told her the children loved to sing all eight verses of "Mary Had a Little Lamb." Eight verses?

Ada rubbed her right shoulder, feeling muscles she'd never felt before.

She was feeling a lot of things she'd never felt before. And not just physically.

Being around Samuel was a balm. At breakfast he'd read from the Bible, and the sound of his mellow voice soothed her and made her happy. They hadn't had a chance to talk in private, yet every time they saw each other, their eyes met and spoke words their mouths couldn't voice.

Ada had purposely stayed behind to help because she wanted time with him. God had opened the door, and she felt good about walking through it. She knew if she went home, *that* world would consume her, and she might melt away like a pad of butter in a hot pan. Plus, if she went back she would have to endure the pressure to marry Owen.

But if she stayed here?

Not once had Samuel said he loved her, or wanted to marry her, or that he wanted her to stay forever. She knew it had only been a day, but time was short. Tonight was Christmas Eve. Tomorrow John would come fetch her, and she would go home and. . .

Ada was drawn from her thoughts when she heard Samuel's boots on the stairs. They needed to talk privately. Now.

She met him in the hallway. "Good afternoon, Ada," he said.

"Samuel."

He held a tray of broth and bread for the sick children. "I heard they're hungry. 'Tis a good sign."

"Yes, it is." She ached to pull him aside and speak with him, to ask him bold questions that would determine her future. But nothing more came out. And he moved on down the hall.

Ada stomped her foot, angry at herself for her own inaction. She looked heavenward. "Please help us. Help me do what *You* want me to do."

Samuel came out of the sickroom. "Ada? Did you say something?"

He'd heard her?

Good.

"I was just praying that God would help us," she said.

He came close. "Help us do what?"

She looked at him, willing him to say something that would reveal his intent. "Tonight is Christmas Eve. I go home tomorrow."

He seemed to struggle to find the words. "I only wish. . ."

"You only wish. . . ?" *Say it plain, Samuel. Please say what I need to hear. Demand that I stay here and marry you. Don't leave me hanging like this.*

"I only wish that you would—"

"Samuel? Is that your voice I hear? I need some help down here."

He answered Eliza's call from the top of the stairs. "Coming."

Suddenly weak at his exit, Ada leaned a shoulder against the doorjamb.

Lord, please help us! Please.

**

Samuel was bursting with words—words he wanted to say, declarations of love he longed to share. With Ada so close, it was heaven.

And it was hell.

Because every time he wanted to speak, he had to hold back because she was betrothed to another.

And yet. . . If that was the case, why wasn't she back home with Owen Reed? If you loved someone, you ached to be with them; you didn't want to miss a moment together. He kept waiting for her to mention Owen. To talk of her engagement—or to talk of a broken engagement.

Something. Anything.

But Ada said nothing. So Samuel could say nothing.

Oh, that she were free! Free to be his wife.

He watched Ada drape popcorn strings around the parlor, knowing that back home her family's Christmas tree was heavy with glass ornaments and lit by a myriad of candles. She sang a carol as she worked, teaching it to the children, one line at a time.

" 'Hark! the herald, angels sing. . .' "

They repeated the line back to her.

"The word's 'sing,' Teddy," she corrected. "Not 'ring.' "

Teddy sang the last word again, making it right.

" 'Glory to the newborn King. . . .' "

Samuel joined in.

Ada beamed.

He committed her face to memory, needing to remember all of this, just in case it was their one and only Christmas together.

**

On Christmas Eve it was time to go to church. Ada helped the children button their coats, none of which fit particularly well, and all of which were tattered hand-me-downs. She noticed Nusa didn't even have a coat, but only a shawl. "No coat?" she asked her.

"I grew too big. This fine," Nusa said and draped it over her head. "See?"

Ada didn't see, but before she could think more about it Samuel clapped his hands. "All ready, children? Everyone hold hands."

They ventured outside to walk to church. A soft snow fell, the perfect accompaniment to the sacred day.

They walked hand in hand, three adults with children in hand or in arms, the oldest children doing their part by taking custody of those younger. The little ones skipped along, their joy overflowing.

Neighbor families came out of their tenements to join the throng, the pleasure of the evening evident on every face.

"Gledelig Jul!"

"Buon Natale!"

"Fröhliche Weihnachten."

"Happy Christmas!"

"Nollaig Shona Dhaoibh."

The greetings in languages understood and foreign added to Ada's happiness. It was as though the entire world were coming together in celebration of Christ's birth.

Outside the church there was a gathering. "What's going on?" Ada asked Samuel.

"They display a nativity scene and place the baby Jesus in the manger on

Christmas Eve. Hurry, so the children can see."

They rushed forward, and the little ones pushed to the front to see a pastor in a black robe reverently place a carved baby Jesus in a small trough, blanketed with straw. Wooden statues of Jesus' father, Joseph, and mother, Mary, looked on. As soon as the baby was settled, the pastor turned with a finger held to his lips. "Shhh. The Christ child is sleeping."

The men removed their hats and one began to sing, " 'Silent night, holy night. . .' "

Everyone joined in, some singing the song in their native tongue.

"Alles schläft; einsam wacht. . ."

"Tu che i Vati da lungi sognar, Tu che angeliche voci nunziar. . ."

"Sov i himmelsæl ro! Sov i himmelsæl ro!"

Ada felt her heart would burst. She'd never experienced such a feeling of unity, nor had she thought much about Jesus belonging to *all*.

In her arms, Francesca ran a finger along the track of Ada's tears. Her little face showed concern. Ada smiled and sang with the crowd. *Help me to always remember this night, Lord. Bless these people. Bless us all.*

Then she spotted Nusa walking out of the crowd toward the manger. The little girl removed her shawl and placed it over the baby Jesus, tucking him in, wiping the snowflakes from Jesus' face.

Nusa returned to Samuel's side, and Samuel pulled her beneath the warmth of his own coat.

Samuel's eyes found Ada's, and he leaned toward her. "She's giving her best to Jesus."

The final verse finished around them.
Jesus, Lord, at Thy birth.
Jesus, Lord, at Thy birth.

**

"She's giving her best to Jesus."

The Christmas Eve service swelled around Ada, yet it was Samuel's words that played over and over in her head.

An eight-year-old little girl who owned nothing of value *but* the shawl, had given that same shawl away.

Ada was moved and humbled, and by Nusa's example began to measure her own heart.

I'm a loving person, a giving person, an empathetic person.

At least she'd thought she was. But until now, had Ada's love, generosity, or empathy ever been truly tested?

Her reverie was interrupted as the offering plate came down the pew. She opened her reticule to gather a donation but was ashamed to see she only had a few coins. She put them all in the plate as it passed by, but knew her "all" was a pittance.

She rationalized that she never carried money. Any item she wished to purchase was bought on the credit of her father's good name. If she was honest, she had little knowledge of the prices of the things she purchased. If she wanted something, she bought it.

Ada looked down at the gold bracelet on her wrist. Impulsively, she pulled it off and leaned over Nusa and Samuel to toss it in the offering plate.

She felt better for it but avoided their eyes. Yes, the bracelet was worth a goodly amount, but still the sacrifice had cost her nothing. Her life would not be changed for the giving of the bracelet — or the keeping of it.

Ada closed her eyes, trying to hold back tears of frustration. She wanted to be a good person. She wanted to do the right thing with the right motives from a loving and grateful heart. She wanted to give her best to Jesus.

Suddenly she thought of her family, at this same moment sitting across town in St. Patrick's Cathedral, dressed in their Christmas finery. She'd sat beside them in church all her life, and yet not once had she thought about putting something in the offering plate when it came by; not once had she thought about sacrificing anything of value. In truth, during the sermon her mind usually strayed to thoughts about how she'd spend Christmas Day, or the new dress she was wanting, or the New Year's Eve party she would attend the coming week.

Frivolous nothings, worth nothing.

I've never given my best to anyone or anything.

She bowed her head, her tears having their way.

Samuel's handkerchief came into view, and she took it, then risked a glance.

"Are you all right?" he whispered.

She started to nod, then gave in to the truth.

"No," she said.

And more than that, she feared she would never be right again.

**

No? She's not all right?

Samuel hated seeing Ada cry. If Nusa weren't sitting between them, he would have put his arm around her shoulders, offering her comfort. He felt so helpless.

Nusa looked up at him with questioning eyes.

Samuel could only smile and nod, suggesting that Ada would be fine.

But would she?

He wasn't sure why she was so upset. The day had gone well, filled with the merriment of the children as they decorated the house, the Christmas Eve dinner of roasted duck and plum pudding, and the happy stroll through the neighborhood to church.

Ada had been happy, too, smiling and offering greetings along the way.

But everything had changed with Nusa's offering of her shawl.

He heard Ada sniff. He ached to talk to her, to understand what had made her so sad.

But until he had that chance, he prayed that God would give her the comfort that he could not.

**

Ada was a good actress. After church she put on a happy face and tucked the children into bed. But the fact that it was her last night here loomed large and heavy.

As soon as she smoothed the covers around Nusa, the little girl asked, "Are you mad I gave shawl?"

"Of course not. It was your shawl to give."

Her brown eyes warmed the room. "I not leave Jesus *kalt*. Not when I have shawl."

Ada looked down at her, so innocent, so giving, so unassuming—all traits *she* should aspire to. A question loomed: Could *she* leave Jesus cold in the snow?

Could she give up what was fine in her life? Could she sacrifice her comfort? Her possessions, her blessings?

"Mama Ada, you all right?"

Ada stroked her cheek. "You humble me, young lady."

Nusa's forehead tightened. She didn't understand.

Ada kissed her forehead and said her own prayer for understanding.

**

Eliza blew out the lamp and settled onto the bed beside Ada. "You go home tomorrow."

"Yes."

"We're going to miss you."

"And I will miss you."

A swath of silence hung between them. "Christmas blessings, Ada."

"The same to you."

Ada did not sleep well that night as the notion of blessings and sacrifice danced in her head.

Chapter Fifteen

The children wiggled and bumped into one another, each trying to find a place to sit at Samuel's feet. In his arms was a huge basket covered with a cloth.

Eliza pointed at Enoch. "Children who shove do not get a Christmas present."

Enoch sat perfectly still—which Samuel knew was quite a feat.

When they were finally settled, Samuel made a show of peeking under the cloth. "Now, what do we have here. . . ?"

He pulled out a carved wooden doll and handed it to Sara Christine. "Mama Eliza made a dress and some hair out of yarn," he said. The doll's arms and legs were tied to the body with a piece of leather, allowing them to move.

The girl touched the doll's face with a mother's tenderness. "Thank you, Papa Samuel."

Next he pulled out a cart and horse. "This is for Siggie."

Siggie spun the wheels. "They work!"

"Of course they work. What good is a cart that can't move?"

"What do you say?" Eliza prodded.

"Thank you, Papa Samuel!"

The rest of the gifts were distributed: a musical clapper for Nusa, a set of wooden blocks for Francesca, a train, some farm animals, another doll, a duck pull toy, a top, a game of nine-pins, a Jacob's ladder, a cup and ball game. . .

Then Samuel gave Eliza her gift. She untied the string holding the towel around it. "It's a pot rack to put on the wall."

"It's beautiful, Samuel," she said.

Samuel looked to Ada. He felt bad for not having a gift for her. "I wish I would have known you were going to be here. I would have made you something."

She sat beside Anthony and helped him spin the top. "No need at all. I had no idea you were so talented. I've never seen toys as fine as these. Ever."

"You're too kind. I—"

There was a knock on the door. Samuel and Ada exchanged a look. Was it John, come to take Ada home? Could Samuel bar the door? Or tell the children to be quiet and pretend no one was home?

"I'll get it," Ada said. She went to the door slowly, as if dreading the task. She paused and took a deep breath; then she opened it. "John. And Owen. I. . .I. . ."

It was clear she hadn't expected Owen. The tone of her voice as she said his name. . . His sudden appearance seemed to distress her.

Distress her? He was her fiancé. She should be happy to see him.

The men stepped in, carrying gifts of holiday food: a ham, spritz cookies, fruit cake, and nuts. Upon recognizing John as the doctor who'd come to help, the children ran to him, showing off their toys. "My, my," he said. "What treasures you have."

As John was drawn away from the door, and Eliza took possession of the food, Ada was left with Owen.

Seeing them together, Samuel felt a swell of panic. But he stepped forward to greet him. "Owen Reed. Merry Christmas to you."

They shook hands. "Samuel Alcott." Owen looked around the room. "So this is where you ended up."

Samuel guessed the comment was not meant as a compliment, but acted otherwise. "We're very proud of the home here. And Miss Wallace has been ever so helpful."

Owen looked at Ada. "I'm very proud of Ada for her charitable nature."

"It's more than charity," she said. "I love helping the children. I love the—"

"I'm sure they'll miss you when you're gone," Owen said.

An awkward silence hung over the room.

Samuel rushed to fill it, to ease Ada's discomfort. "Congratulations on your upcoming marriage, Owen," he said.

"Thank you," Owen said. "We're both looking forward to it, aren't we, Ada?"

Ada was staring at Samuel, her face distraught. She looked as if she wanted him to save her. And more than anything he wanted to save her, to pull her into his arms and say, "You can't marry her. *I'm* going to marry her!"

But then John interrupted and retrieved Ada's wool cape from a hook by the door. "Come now, sister. Our parents are waiting for your return so we can celebrate our own Christmas."

Although Owen leaned close to Ada and spoke in a whisper, Samuel heard his words. "I've bought you the most lavish present."

And there it was. Owen could offer Ada a life full of lavish presents. And here, today, Samuel had had nothing to give her for Christmas.

In a flurry of activity, Ada's coat was helped on, her bonnet tied, and the children kissed. As the door opened, Samuel panicked. For once she went through that door, she would be gone to him forever.

He stepped through the crowd of children. "Ada? Miss Wallace?"

She turned to him, her eyes frightened and confused. "Yes, Samuel?"

"I. . ." He didn't know how to say what needed to be said.

Owen took her hand. "Come, Ada. The carriage is waiting."

With one last look, she turned and left him.

The door closed, shutting her off from him forever.

**

The carriage ride home was accompanied by much talking—by her brother and Owen. Ada heard a phrase here and there, and even responded in a fashion, but her mind was absorbed with one thought: Samuel knew that she and Owen were engaged?

How did he know about the engagement?

How long had he known?

Although she would have liked to know the details, the point remained that he *did* know. And with her knowledge of *his* knowledge came new eyes regarding Samuel's recent behavior: his reserve, his awful politeness, and their limited snippets of personal connection.

If only he'd said something to her earlier. If only he'd congratulated her on her engagement, or mentioned it in some way, she could have told him the whole awkward story of her betrothal.

Yet by telling him the truth, she would have virtually been asking him. . .suggesting to him that they. . .

Did Samuel want to marry her?

John's voice intruded. "You should see the spread Mother has planned for Christmas dinner. Goose and turkey, yams and hard rolls, cranberry relish, minced meat *and* pecan pies."

Ada put a hand to her mouth. The thought of eating disturbed more than enticed.

"Aren't you feeling well, Ada?" Owen asked.

Perhaps if she feigned illness, once she got home she could escape to her room and wallow in her thoughts and memories of Samuel. And she needed time to pray, to talk to God, to ask Him if this was really what He wanted. How could this be His plan for her life when it made her feel so dreadful?

"Oh, Ada's fine," John said. "When she sees the Christmas tree and has a cup of wassail, she'll be her old self again."

But Ada didn't want to be her old self.

**

"Papa Samuel, will you read?" Nusa held a copy of *Hans Brinker and the Silver Skates*.

Eliza rushed forward to shoo the girl away. "Leave Samuel alone, Nusa. He needs some time to himself."

Samuel was glad for the intervention. Since Ada's departure he'd been tormented by a bevy of should-have-saids and should-have-dones. His first inclination had been to run after the carriage, calling, "Ada! Come back! Come back!"

Nusa stood before Samuel, studying him.

"Please, Nusa. . ."

"Why you not stop Mama Ada from going?"

Good question. "She's supposed to marry Mr. Reed."

Nusa shook her head. "She supposed to marry you. Marry us."

And there it was. The truth laid out as fact.

"Now, Samuel. Now."

God's words. He'd heard them before and had only partially followed through. But God didn't want partial obedience. Partial faith. He wanted people to step out boldly, to trust Him completely. Samuel had asked for guidance. *Had* God spoken to him?

There was only one way to know for sure.

He stood.

"You go get her?" Nusa asked.

Could he do that? Could he rush to the Wallace house, knock on the door, and claim Ada as his own?

"Should I?" Samuel asked, even though he knew the answer.

"Of course," Nusa said, in that simple way of children. "God brought her here. To us. He want her here."

Samuel smiled. "He does?"

Nusa's nod was strong. Then she ran to get Samuel's coat. "Can I go, too?"

"Not this time, Nusa. This, I have to do alone."

But not alone. For finally, at this moment, Samuel was certain God had been with him—had been with both of them— since the first moment he and Ada had met. Each happenstance since had been set in place by their heavenly Father. Though both he and Ada had been offered choices along the way, with this final choice made,

Samuel felt as though he was finally and firmly rooted in the Almighty's plan.

Which, as always, was the best plan.

**

Ada sat in the drawing room of her family's home, an immense Christmas tree decorated in the corner, the candles making it glow like the stars in a Bethlehem sky. A fire roared in the fireplace, and the smell of spiced cider and pine boughs filled the room.

Nana untied the ribbon around a quilted bed jacket Ada had made for her. She held the item close, inspecting the stitches. "You are so talented at quilting and embroidery, child. It's beautiful."

Ada's mother chimed in. "Now that you're quilting again, once you choose the fabric for your wedding gown, you'll be able to finally finish your bridal quilt."

Ada thought about the unfinished quilt. The satin of a wedding dress she'd wear to marry Owen did not fit with the rest of the quilt, which chronicled her life before Samuel, and finally with him. What came after Samuel had no place on the quilt, no right to be there. Just as the quilt had stopped, so had her life. It was as though there'd been a gap in time. The months and days since Samuel had left her last Christmas until he'd come back to her a few weeks ago were a blur, as if she'd been sleepwalking, waiting to be awakened.

But now she *was* fully awake. In this clarity she knew what needed to be done, and prayed she had the strength to do it.

Owen stood and handed her a gift. "This is from me," he said.

He was clearly excited to see her open it, yet that was the last thing she wanted to do. To open it would add another slice of time to her Owen-life.

"Ada," Father said. "Don't keep Owen waiting."

She had no choice but to untie the ribbon and open the velvet box.

"They're emeralds," Owen said proudly. "The set belonged to my mother, but she — but I — want you to have it."

Ada touched the largest stone at the climax of the substantial necklace. There were three-stone drop earrings and a matching bracelet.

Mother came to her side to admire it. "Oh, Owen. This is exquisite."

"It's only the beginning. Although I wanted to give you family jewels for this first Christmas together, I promise to have some modern pieces made for you in the future. We'll go to Tiffany's together, and you can choose whatever stones and setting you like."

"You are too generous," Mother said. "Come now, Ada, you must try it on."

Ada didn't want the emeralds to touch her skin. For once they did, she felt as if she would be branded: forever Owen's. The emeralds would sear into her skin and—

I'm not Owen's. I'm Samuel's. With my entire being I belong to Samuel! Lord, please give me the strength to do what I must do.

There was a knock on the door.

Ada's heart jumped to her throat. She gave her mother possession of the emeralds and stood.

"Who would come calling on Christmas?" her father asked.

Is it. . . ? Could it be. . . ? Please let it be. . .

Ada took a step toward the foyer, but Mother put a hand on her arm and kept her back. "Wilson will get it, dear. Come now and let's put on the necklace."

Ada heard a man's voice talking to the butler. And then the butler led him in.

"Mr. Alcott, sir. Ma'am," Wilson announced.

And suddenly her family was gone from the room. Gone from the world. Only two people existed: Ada and her Samuel.

She ran to him and pulled him close. "Oh, Samuel, I prayed you'd come."

He whispered in her ear. "I never should have let you go."

Ada's mother was in a panic. "Ada! What are you doing? Let go of him! Come back here with your family."

Ada released Samuel but for an arm around his waist. "Samuel is my family, Mother."

"He most certainly is not. Don't be ridiculous." She turned to the others in the drawing room, who stood staring at the scene. "Horace. John. Owen. Mother. Stop her."

"Ada seems to know her own mind," Nana said softly.

Mother looked aghast and turned to Owen. "Owen, please. She's to be your wife."

Owen looked uneasy but took a step forward. "Is she?" He looked at Ada, his brow furrowed. "Are you, Ada? Are you going to be my wife?"

This was the hard part. To choose one man, she must hurt another. Reluctantly she left Samuel and took Owen's hand in hers. "Owen, you are a wonderful man and will make someone very happy."

"I want to make you very happy."

She shook her head. "But I would not make *you* happy. You deserve a wife who will adore and cherish you. I am not that woman."

For the first time, Ada's father spoke up. "This is ridiculous, daughter. You can't break your engagement to Owen. His father and I agreed—"

Mother interrupted. "His mother and I agreed. And wedding arrangements have begun."

"Hush, both of you," Nana said. "None of that matters."

"Of course it matters," Mother said.

Ada agreed with Nana. It was time to focus on what *did* matter.

Suddenly an image of Nusa offering her best to the baby Jesus came to her mind. *"What will you offer Me? What is your best?"*

Where was Ada at her best? Where were the best parts of her — her giving nature, her compassion, and her ability to love — allowed to flourish?

It was not here, in the lush drawing room of a mansion on Fifth Avenue.

"Surrender yourself as you are, and I will help you be your best."

Ada pulled in a breath, the thoughts, the inner voice vivid in her mind. For her Christmas gift Nusa had given Jesus all she had. For Ada's Christmas gift. . .

She closed her eyes, needing to concentrate on this very important offering. *I give You my life, Lord. I offer my life to You, for You to do with as You will.*

And suddenly she felt a calling from God. And with it came the knowledge that it had always been there, an unopened gift, waiting for her to unwrap His glorious will.

"Ada?" Mother said. "Don't just stand there with your eyes closed. Do something."

Ada opened her eyes and smiled, knowing that she *had* done something, *the* something that would change everything.

A wave of peace passed over her, letting her know that God had accepted her offering — and approved. "Please forgive me," she said to Owen and her family. "But everything has changed. I'm not who I used to be, nor am I the woman I'm going to be. I only know that God has opened a door, and I'm walking through it."

"Door?" her father said. "What door?"

She looked to Samuel. "The door that leads me to Samuel."

Oddly, it was Owen who spoke next. "Do you love him, Ada?"

Ada's eyes remained on Samuel. She hated that the first time she'd say the words she was across the room from him. But perhaps it was necessary. She held her ground but kept her eyes on his. "Oh yes."

He beamed and held out his hand.

She crossed the room, leaving one man's hand to take up another's. And once again, they were alone in the world.

Samuel beamed down at her. "Remember how I said I had nothing to offer you this Christmas? Actually, I do. I give you my hands to provide for you, my arms to hold you and keep you safe, my eyes to see who you really are, my ears to listen to your thoughts and desires, my lips to say I love you, and my heart to swell with joy at your presence. I give you all of myself. And so. . ." He got down on one knee. "Ada, my love, will you be my wife?"

Ada spoke with utter confidence. "Yes, oh yes."

She fell into his arms.

Where she belonged.

Epilogue

One year later

"Nusa! You're eating more popcorn than you're stringing," Ada said as she and the children sat around the kitchen table making Christmas garlands.

Nusa merely smiled and put a garland around Ada's neck. "A Christmas necklace," she said. "And you can eat it, too."

The children laughed, and Ada found their laughter more precious than jewels.

Then she heard Samuel and his grandfather coming down the stairs, talking about the just completed addition to the foundling home. She moved to join them. "I'll see if I can get a couple more oak dressers sent over from Macy's," Mr. Alcott said. "One for the older boys' room and one for the new baby."

"That's very generous of you, Grandfather," Samuel said. "Generous again. Buying the building next door and helping us expand. . ." He looked at his wife. "And I know for a fact that both Ada

233

and I are much appreciative of having our own apartment there."

"I admit it's better than the attic room," Ada said with a laugh.

"I still wish you would have agreed to turn my home into an orphanage," Mr. Alcott said. "All those empty rooms going to waste."

Ada kissed him on the cheek. "Your offer was extremely generous, but we need to be down here in Five Points, so the children can find us."

A little three-year-old tugged on Mr. Alcott's coat. He picked her up. "Yes, well. . .there is that."

"And don't offer up our house so quickly," Nana said as she came down the stairs. "As your wife, I have plans to use that space for charity fund-raisers and women's suffrage rallies and — "

"You'll drive me to drink, dear woman," Mr. Alcott said.

She reached the foyer and flicked the tip of his nose. "I drive you to *think*. And you love it."

"That I do," he said.

Ada found a place beneath Samuel's arm and rested a hand on her ample belly.

She felt the baby move, low and heavy. With any luck, it could still be a Christmas baby. So many events of their lives linked to Christmas. . . .

Eliza appeared at the top of the stairs and called down to Ada. "Your surprise is ready. You can send the children up now."

Finally. After months of work, her Christmas present was complete.

Ada went back to the kitchen to gather the children. "Are you ready for your Christmas gifts?"

"Yes!"

"Yay!"

Ada crooked a finger at them. "Follow me."

They scrambled around her, a thundering herd following her up the stairs. Once on the landing she set them loose to scatter to the bedrooms.

Exclamations, shouts, and laughter erupted. Ada was joined by the other adults, and they walked from room to room. The children came and went between them, excited about their gifts.

Her brother, John, came out of the boys' bedroom, laughing at the melee. "Mother will be appalled you cut it up."

"She knows, and she *was* appalled. But she came to understand. For what better use of my bridal quilt than to embellish the coverlets of my children. By the way, brother, are you coming over for Christmas dinner tomorrow? Mother and Father are coming around one."

John nodded, and they all watched as the children examined their new coverlets that were each adorned by a portion of her quilt, the quilt that showcased the costumes of Ada's life, the gowns and dresses that had once seemed so important to her. Many coverlets made from one. Ada loved the symbolism of it. She had been one girl, concerned with only herself. And now, through love, her life had expanded a hundredfold.

Ada had one more surprise and, from behind a door, pulled out a pillow that highlighted a very important part of her quilt. She handed it to Samuel.

"This is for you. I started it last year, but now it's finally finished."

He ran his fingers along a patch of rough cloth, its textures intermixed with the finer silks and brocades. "These are from my shirt," he said. "The one I was wearing on the day of the accident."

Ada nodded and continued his tour. "And this is from the dress I wore that first day I saw you in Five Points, and this, from the dress I wore when we brought you home, and this green is from the dress I wore when I came back to help the sick children, and—"

"And this red velvet is from the dress you were wearing when I came to your house and proposed."

"And I said yes." They kissed across the pillow.

So many days. So many memories. But as they looked at the joyful children bustling around them and their happy grandparents reunited in love, Ada knew that the waiting had been worth it.

For *now* was the most wonderful time of the year.

THE END

Discussion Questions

1. Ava is very close to her grandmother. She's someone she can confide in and be herself with. Who fills these needs in your life?

2. Ava's quilt is a chronicle of her life. Do you do anything to chronicle your life? A diary, scrapbooks? What other ways could you record the moments of your life?

3. Samuel is drawn into going down to Five Points to go "slumming" with his friends. What situation have your friends drawn you into? What are ways you could have told them no?

4. Samuel feels an inner voice directing him, and he takes this voice to be God giving him direction. How does God speak to you?

5. Samuel takes a huge risk saving Nusa *and* bringing her home. The choice changed his life completely. When has

your life been changed by an act of kindness—from you or done for you?

6. Samuel feels an instant connection when he's at the Merciful Children Foundling Home. When have you felt a strong connection to a place, an organization, or a group of people? Why?

7. Samuel sees a need at the Foundling Home but has no money to spare until his grandfather gives him a ring, freeing up Samuel's money. When has God provided finances to you at just the right time?

8. Do you agree with Samuel's decision to break up with Ava? How do you think the story would have ended if he'd stayed with her the first time?

9. You are the casting director for the film version of *The Bridal Quilt*. Who would you cast to play Ava? Samuel? Eliza? Owen?

10. If you were in charge of writing epitaphs for these characters, what would you say about them?

About the Author

NANCY MOSER is the best-selling author of over 40 novels, novellas, and children's books, including Christy Award winner *Time Lottery* and Christy finalist *Washington's Lady*. She's written seventeen historical novels including *Love of the Summerfields, Masquerade, Where Time Will Take Me*, and *Just Jane. An Unlikely Suitor* was named to Booklist's "Top 100 Romance Novels of the Decade." *The Pattern Artist* was a finalist in the Romantic Times Reviewers Choice award. Some of her contemporary novels are: *An Undiscovered Life, The Invitation, Solemnly Swear, The Good Nearby, John 3:16, Crossroads, The Seat Beside Me*, and the Sister Circle series. *Eyes of Our Heart* was a finalist in the Faith, Hope, and Love Readers' Choice Awards. Nancy has been married for over 45 years — to the same man. She and her husband have three grown children, seven grandchildren, and live in the Midwest. She's been blessed with a varied life. She's earned a degree in architecture, run a business with her husband, traveled extensively in Europe, and has performed in various theaters, symphonies, and choirs. She knits voraciously, kills all her houseplants, and can wire an electrical fixture without getting shocked. She is a fan of anything antique — humans included.

Website: www.nancymoser.com
Blogs: Author blog:
www.authornancymoser.blogspot.com
History blog:
www.footnotesfromhistory.blogspot.com
Facebook:
www.facebook.com/nancymoser.author
Bookbub:
www.bookbub.com/authors/nancy-moser?list=author_ books
Goodreads:
www.goodreads.com/author/show/117288.Nancy_Moser
Pinterest:
www.pinterest.com/nancymoser1/_saved/
Instagram: www.instagram.com/nmoser33/

If you would like to read other Gilded Age stories,
read the Gilded Age Series:
Masquerade and *An Unlikely Suitor*

Excerpt from *Masquerade*

Dornby Manor
Wiltshire, England
Early autumn 1886

"I've told you, Father, I won't marry him."

Thomas Gleason held a matchstick to the bowl of his pipe and puffed repeatedly, luring the tobacco to ignite. "It's a good match, daughter. Everyone has heard of the Tremaines, even here in England."

Heard of their money, perhaps . . .

Lottie remembered the whispered rumors about the Tremaines. She knew her parents hated gossip — or pretended to for propriety's sake — but now was not the time for her to be timid. "Some say the Tremaines are *nouveau riche.* The elder Mr. Tremaine is but one generation away from those who peddled their goods on the streets of New York City."

Her father pointed his pipe at her. "Perhaps. But Tremaine's Dry Goods has grown to encompass a five-story building, taking up an entire city block."

Mother shook her head and said beneath her breath, "A glorified shopkeeper."

Father shot her a glance.

Mother nodded to the maid, Dora, to pour the tea. "We are the ones doing the Tremaines the favor. You are Sir Thomas Gleason," she said. "The Gleasons have ties to Richard the Second. Our name is listed in *Debrett's.*"

A puff of smoke billowed in front of Father's face. "Now, now, Hester. By seeking a goodly match for our daughter, we're not negating our own roots. It's a blessing the Tremaines have shown interest in our Charlotte, especially since they've never met any of us. And considering . . . "

Lottie interrupted. "You act as if meeting me might cause them to change their minds. I may not be a ravishing beauty, Father, but I've been complimented many times regarding my appearance."

"No, no," her father said. "Don't take offense. You're a lovely girl. I was merely pointing out the odd circumstances of . . . our situation."

Hester coughed and put her ever-present handkerchief to her mouth.

Lottie tried unsuccessfully to squelch her annoyance at her mother's cough. Hack, hack, hack. Perhaps if Mother spent more time outside, walking the grounds of their Wiltshire estate, her health would improve. But Mother prided herself on indoor pursuits, namely her needlepoint chair cushions. Best in the county, she bragged. Lottie didn't care for such nonsense. To go to so much work only to have someone sit upon it was absurd.

As was this conversation.

Lottie set her teacup down, rose from her chair, and moved to the windows that overlooked the front lawn. "I don't see why we have to talk about this now." *Or ever.* "It's my birthday and my friends will be arriving for my party soon and . . . " She turned to her mother directly. "Speaking of my party, why aren't you bustling about? A dozen of my friends will arrive in just a few hours, yet if I didn't know better, I'd think the party was next Tuesday rather than today."

The handkerchief rose once again. "You said you didn't want an extravagant soiree, dear, just a light repast with cakes and sweets for your friends. Mrs. Movery is quite busy with the food preparations, I'm sure." She glanced at Dora. "In fact, toward that end . . .

Dora, why don't you go see how things are coming along in the kitchen."

Dora said, "Yes, ma'am," and left them.

Lottie wished she would have stayed. Dora was her lady's maid and her best friend in the entire world. But lately, her parents had started asking Dora to do other tasks, even helping out in the kitchen, which was unthinkable. Lottie *had* noticed a few of the housemaids and parlor--maids were no longer in service with the family, but that didn't mean Dora should suffer. "I don't understand why Dora is suddenly being asked to expand her duties. She's *my* maid. I assure you I keep her very busy."

"I'm sure you do, daughter," her father said. "But, well . . . "

Mother continued the thought. "With the preparations for your party this afternoon . . . "

Something wasn't being said. Lottie wished her parents would tell her what was going on. She had a good mind. She could practically recite the novels of Jane Austen and the Brontë sisters by heart. Didn't that prove she had an intellect worth utilizing? Sometimes Lottie thought she would scream from lack of purpose. To sit in the house all day, reading or doing needlework, waiting for someone of consequence to call was silly. She would happily trade two women of means for one person who could offer amusement or witty conversation. Odd how those attributes were sorely lacking in polite society, among people who were far too polite to be of interest.

But now, looking out upon the front drive and the vista of the green that carpeted the house to the road, she abandoned her worries for the anticipation of seeing carriage after carriage arriving for her party. Guests laden with presents — for her. Perhaps purpose was overrated. In all her nineteen years she'd found it quite acceptable — pleasant, really — to let the world beyond their country home dip and spin without her. What did she care of labor acts or problems in Ireland or whether Queen Victoria became Empress of Burma? Where in the world was Burma?

Lottie preferred experiencing life through novels where the characters were always enjoying a lovely ball or romp through the countryside that would lead them to their one true love. Her copies of *Pride & Prejudice, Sense & Sensibility,* and *Little Women* were threadbare. Lottie especially enjoyed stories about sisters — perhaps because she had none. Conversely, she did not enjoy the books of Elizabeth Gaskell or Charles Dickens with the same zeal, finding their stories too driven by social inequities. She didn't want to read about the world's problems. She wanted romance, diversion, passion, and a happy ending — in her books *and* in real life.

And yet, she also wanted to feel of *use*. There was a stirring inside that niggled like an empty stomach demanding *something* of her. From her. When she felt such discontent she usually sought the outdoors where the movement of her body and the addition of fresh air were a good counter to her restlessness. Until she could pinpoint the answer to this inner unrest, she planned on marrying well and setting up her own home in a nearby estate.

Surely true love would be the key to unlocking her true purpose. But marrying an American as her parents suggested? There could be no key in that. Even if he was rich, he would never understand her inner need, and she'd be held in bondage, far from family and friends and the dream she had of becoming . . .

Something. Someone.

Her mother interrupted her thoughts. "Conrad Tremaine seems to be a very nice young man."

In this context, *nice* was a lethal word, one that was used when better words like *dashing, handsome,* and *debonair* did not apply. Judging from the letters Lottie had received from the *nice* Mr. Tremaine, along with the small photograph . . . She'd read the letters many times and had dissected the photograph with her father's magnifying glass, but no matter how hard she looked at his representation in either word or countenance, Mr. Tremaine was no Mr. Darcy. Or Willoughby. Or even Heathcliff. He came off sounding stumbling in the first and looking bumbling in the latter.

And pudgy. With a weakish chin. And a hairline that promised to recede into nothingness sooner rather than later.

Apparently not knowing what else to say, her father repeated his mantra: "It's a good match, daughter."

Lottie suffered a shiver of disgust. Her parents had endured an arranged marriage—with emphasis on the word *endured*—and now they expected her to do the same? Although they put up a good front, Lottie recognized her mother's stern and pinched appearance to be the consequence of enduring rather than enjoying her life. Lottie had become cognizant of it a few years previous when she'd looked more closely at her parents' wedding photograph. She'd been shocked to find little resemblance between the sweet expectation upon her mother's face and the dour mask that existed now. Did expectation of *any* sort remain behind that mask? Or had it been extinguished through a union that was false in all aspects but the law?

And her father . . . his countenance had not changed, nor had his pre-marriage behavior. He was unfaithful. His longtime mistress, Mrs. Lancashire, lived in Bath, just thirteen short miles away. Certainly Mother knew, for she had long ago refused to go to Bath, even though the medicinal benefits of its spas might have helped her chronic health issues.

Lottie had seen this mistress once, at age twelve, when she'd accompanied her father to that city. Lottie had known nothing of his weaknesses before the trip. But as a young person just awakening to the world of adult desires, her eyes and ears were aware of lingering looks and hushed rumors about her father and "another woman." When Lottie finally saw her, she found Mrs. Lancashire to be a pretty thing, yet rather mindless in that she laughed too much and too loudly. At the gathering, Mrs. Lancashire had been accompanied by her husband, which had been confusing, considering the rumors. Nanny had tried to explain to Lottie the truth of things as best she could. It was the first time Lottie had ever heard the word *adultery* — the seventh Commandment come to life.

After she returned from that trip, Lottie had vowed she would never, ever marry without love. And she would never, ever place herself in a situation where she would have to be the understanding wife to her husband's indiscretions. She would never, ever —

The butler entered the room with several letters on a silver tray, and Mother perked up at the diversion. "Oh, lovely. The post has arrived." She extended the top letter toward Lottie. "I recognize this handwriting. Conrad's ears must have been burning."

Lottie abandoned the vista of the window, retrieved the letter, and opened it.

"Come now, daughter. Show some enthusiasm. What does Conrad have to say?" her father asked.

Lottie scanned the lines to find something of interest, but the words merged into inane dribble and drabble. "He extends his greetings and those of his parents."

"How very nice." Hester nodded to her husband. "We ask that you extend the same to his family in your next correspondence."

Bland niceties sent across the sea. As passionless and unappealing as milk toast.

Or tea. Lottie returned to her chair and took a sip. She'd never liked tea much. And after reading the American novel *Little Women,* she'd tried coffee and had liked both the beverage and the book very much. Those working-class American girls were always drinking coffee, having adventures, and feeling free and loved. Oh, to have three sisters, three confidantes. Lottie had a handful of female friends here in Wiltshire, but none in whom she could fully confide. The only friend she could count on was her lady's maid, Dora. But it wasn't the same as having a true sister.

Lottie had never found the courage to ask her mother why she had no siblings... (continued)

Purchase *Masquerade* on Amazon

Made in United States
North Haven, CT
22 March 2022